UFO's – Sightings Reports - Cover-ups

William G. Weber
With
Maj. George A. Filer, USAF (Ret.)

Copyright © 2024

All Rights Reserved

ISBN: 978-1-963919-19-6

Dedication

To my wife and best friend, Deborah, for her belief, patience, and support in encouraging me to write this book.

To my boys, Christopher and Brian, for always believing in me.

To the sighting witnesses who came forward to share their experiences and tell their stories.

Acknowledgment

I would like to acknowledge the people listed below:

Maj. George A. Filer III USAF (retired) for his contributions in the Ft. Dix / McGuire AFB and Pine Bush Chapters

MUFON Investigators: Dan Medleycott, Karen Calvacca and Dr. Nick Platco for their valuable contributions in the Bethlehem, Mountain Top and Coatesville Chapters

Contents

Dedication	iv
Acknowledgment	vi
About the Author	x
Forward	xii
In the beginning…	1
References	19
The Year is 1965	20
References	41
Carbondale, PA UFO Incident – 1974	42
References	64
Incident at Joint Base McGuire/Dix/Lakehurst	65
Lukens Steel - Coatesville, PA – 1992 Incident	164
Pine Bush, NY - 1997	169
Sighting at Bethlehem, PA - 2013	183
Sighting at Mountain Top, PA – 2016	209
UFOs & Technology: What Influence Did They Have?	220
The Denial Still Continues	240
References	242
Glossary of Terms	243

About the Author

Bill Weber, currently living in a suburb of Philadelphia, has always been interested in science. He has explored how and why things in everyday life work. With a background in Electrical Engineering, he has been granted three U.S. Patents. Fascinated by space and the possibility of extraterrestrial life, he joined an organization called MUFON, which was founded in 1969 shortly after the USAF shut down Project Bluebook. MUFON stands for the Mutual UFO Network. Over the 26-plus years he has been with them, he has held several positions, ranging from Certified Field Investigator to State Director for both Pennsylvania and Delaware. In these roles, he investigated over 100 cases, including anomalous lights, orbs, crop circles, UAPs, and possible abduction cases. As State Director, he was responsible for a team of Certified Field Investigators and their leaders. He was also a member of the STAR team, similar to MUFON's SWAT team.

Bill presented his research at the MUFON 2011, 2013, and 2017 PA State Conferences. Additionally, he presented his material at several Main Line MUFON events, UFO Awareness Days, and conferences in New Jersey, Connecticut, and multiple state libraries. He appeared as a guest speaker on the WHFR/FM radio show "We Are Not Alone" from the Dearborn/Detroit, MI area, and also on the "Late Night in the Midlands" radio show from Columbia, S.C. Bill was the guest speaker on the "UFOs Over Pennsylvania" TV show, which aired on PCTV 21 Pittsburgh, PA. Finally, he was the guest speaker at the History/Mystery event held in Essington, PA in October 2015.

No longer with MUFON, Bill now spends his time conducting his own research, which has inspired him to write this book. It's important to note that this book will contain actual documented cases from Pennsylvania, New York, and New Jersey, where Bill was directly involved in some of the investigations.

The author also has a private group for discussion on Facebook. The Facebook group page is **Del-Val Ufology Interest Group.**

Forward

Social media has revolutionized the dissemination of data. It has affected how individuals research and investigate UFO sightings, alien abductions, and alien close encounter events. Social media posts, videos, podcasts, and personal or news websites provide information that otherwise would not have been easily, if at all, available to ufologists in the past. The instant dissemination of a recent Unknown Aerial Vehicle (UAV) or Unknown Aerial Phenomena (UAP) sighting provides researchers and investigators with relevant and timely data they can apply to their own projects. The release of documents related to ufology is spread across the Internet to be used as evidence or a source in an investigation, research paper, or book. The internet, like it or hate it, has had a transformative effect on the field of ufology.

This book is a hybrid of internet research, written primary and secondary sources, and oral history. All three form the foundation of a proper UFO sighting, alien abduction, or alien sighting investigation. Bill Weber and George Filer work together to document the life and UFO experiences George had as a military officer. Bill goes on to document and explain some of the most compelling UFO sightings and events in the field and during his time as a UFO investigator. His review of an event's or investigation's context as well as conclusions are rare in more recent books about this field. This book is a great resource for new or seasoned members of this field to use as a springboard to further their own avenues of study in ufology.

Michael Panicello

UFO Researcher and Investigator.

UFO'S – SIGHTINGS---REPORTS - COVER-UPS

In the beginning...

UFOs (Unidentified Flying Objects), or as they are now called UAPs (Unidentified Aerial Phenomena), have been around and with us for a long, long time. These objects have been seen in many parts of the world over the centuries. A majority of the time, they generate fear and doubt as to what is being witnessed, and in some cases, they were worshiped as gods. One of the earliest sightings was documented in the writings of the ancient Greek historian Diodorus Siculus Timoleon, while he was traveling from Corinth to Sicily around 343 BC. This was witnessed while he was traveling from Corinth to Sicily. [1]

There were many sightings of strange aerial phenomena during the Second Punic War between 218 and 201 BC. Rome's governmental records, the Annales Maximi, would tell of several of them. In 218 BC, there were reports of ships which gleamed in the sky coming out of the clouds. Two years later, in 216 BC, came a similar sighting of "gleaming round shields" traveling through the air. [2]

Christopher Columbus had an encounter, which he recorded in his log prior to discovering land back on October 11, 1492, at 10:00 PM. He, in fact, had summoned some crew members to see what he was seeing. Columbus had stated that while he was on the deck of the Santa Maria, he saw a light, similar to the light from a candle, moving up and down, following their ship.

He indicated that the light had risen up from the water and climbed up into the atmosphere. [3]

On April 14th, 1561, residents of the bustling Bavarian town of Nuremberg woke up to a frightening scene. Hundreds of little fireballs were exploding in the sky, and crafts of all shapes and sizes—spheres, triangles, cylinders, and crosses—were whizzing past each other. Spheroid UFOs were seen emerging from cylindrical ships and darting across the sky erratically and clashing with each other in a colossal aerial battle that lasted for over an hour. Eventually, a large black triangular object appeared, and then a large crash was heard outside of the city. The reports of the event say it lasted for about an hour, and artist Hans Glaser documented this strange event for the German Nuremberg Gazette (shown below). Describing the event, he refers to crosses, tubes, wheels, multi-colored objects, and globes over the city—hundreds of them. Objects would disappear in smoke, some even crashing into the ground. The smoke was visible for miles. [4]

It has been said that at the end of the day, the Nuremberg 1561 event was not a battle of alien spaceships but a series of unusual weather events that were given a religious tone and sensationalized by Hans Glaser, because of poor understanding as well as to feed the public's hunger for outrageous stories. [4] *Or, was this a typical cover-up at the time to squelch fear of the unknown and the story?*

UFO'S – SIGHTINGS---REPORTS - COVER-UPS

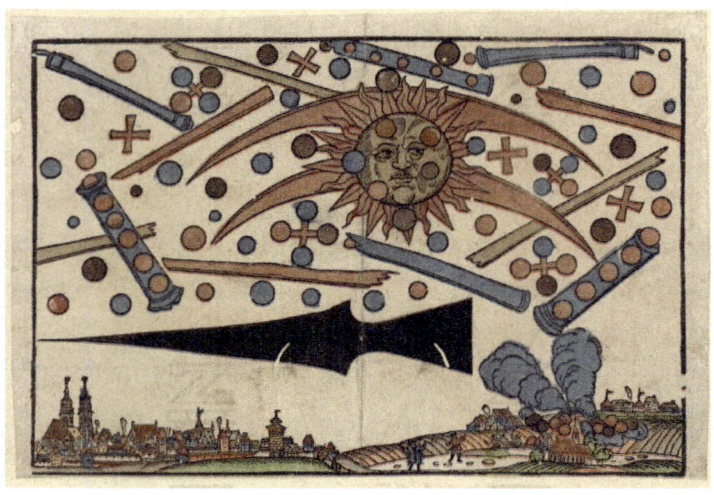

Broadsheet of alleged Nuremburg event.

    The most remarkable thing about this account was the fact that it wasn't the only one recorded. On August 7, 1566, after the Nuremberg spectacle, an almost identical sighting was made in the skies of the Swiss city of Basel. Dark spheres were witnessed hovering over the town of Basel, Switzerland in 1566. The spheres appeared at sunrise. *'Many became red and fiery, ending by being consumed and vanishing,'* wrote Samuel Coccius in the local newspaper on this date. [5]

16th century woodcut of spheres seen over Basel, Switzerland, August 7, 1566. (Wickiana Collection, Zurich Central Library)

Moving forward, did a cigar-shaped unidentified flying object really crash near Aurora, Texas, on April 19, 1897? Some people believe the whole story was a fabrication by S. E. Hayden, a local cotton buyer, while others are reasonably sure the tragic accident really occurred. Investigators from the Mutual UFD Network, headquartered in Seguin, Texas, have uncovered evidence that raises doubts about the hoax theory. Sightings of strange airships were reported all across the United States during the spring of 1897. Was the Aurora incident just another UFO sighting, but with an unusual twist?

It resulted in the allegation that an object crashed and left debris as proof of the event. Bill Case, a State Director for the

UFO'S – SIGHTINGS---REPORTS - COVER-UPS

Mutual UFO Network, discovered family members of the original witnesses were ready to tell what happened that memorable day. Mrs. Mary Evans, about 15 years old at the time, said her mother and father went to the crash site and told her how the airship had exploded and that the pilot was torn up and killed in the crash. He was a small man and was buried later that day in the local cemetery by the men of the town. Jim Stephens told his son Charlie how the nose of the airship hit the windmill over the water well on Judge J. S. Proctor's farm causing a chain reaction explosion. The flash followed by a fire was visible for more than three miles. Investigators have reconstructed the events of the sighting and located the crash site. Using sophisticated metal detecting equipment and guided by the eyewitness accounts, they retrieved pieces of metal of various sizes and types. Bill Case said, "From all indications, there was definitely an explosion.

The pattern established by metals recovered indicates the craft exploded on the lower right side, first blowing bits and pieces over a two or three-acre area east and northeast of the well site on top of a rocky limestone hill. Immediately, the rest of the craft exploded throwing other samples to the north and west." Although it is difficult to determine which samples may have resulted from the crash, as compared with debris left by people living on the farm during the past three-quarters of a century, some of the samples were unique. One piece, thought to be a structural member of some kind, was analyzed by a major U.S. laboratory with exciting results. An electron dispersion X-ray analyzer was used to identify the elements found in the sample. Only aluminum with a trace of iron could be detected. The sample was retrieved from a location about 100 feet west of the well site beneath four inches of soil. It was lodged directly against the face of the limestone rock and conformed to the exact configuration of the stone, indicating it was in a near molten state when it penetrated the earth and hit the rock where it cooled. X-ray fluorescence analysis determined the sample to be free of zinc. This was an unexpected finding, since the samples retrieved from the east of the well site contained zinc. The soft X-ray spectrographic analysis verified the high purity of the aluminum, the inclusion of iron, and the absence of copper. This also is an anomaly, because commercial aluminum alloys that contain iron usually contain copper.

Photomicrographs of the sample show the presence of large grains, indicating the sample is stress-free and has gone through a melting and cooling stage. Details of the analysis provide additional clues as to how the material was constructed, the nature of the crystalline structure, and unusual purity. All this is consistent with the allegation that an object exploded spewing debris in all directions, impacting with tremendous force. Investigators were able to locate a crude headstone marking a grave in the local cemetery. Metal detecting equipment gave the same readings at the gravesite as they did where the metal was found. The marker and the detector readings seemed to be sufficient for investigators to demand the opening of the grave and exhumation of the pilot's body. Local citizens didn't agree. They blocked the opening of the grave. Soon thereafter, the headstone was removed, and the grave left unmarked and anonymous. Perhaps the people of Aurora were afraid their longstanding popularity would be diminished if the grave was opened and science proved the whole event was a hoax. On the other hand, what if the grave did hold the remains of an alien pilot? At this time, the investigators' files hold sufficient evidence to cast reasonable doubt on the hoax theory. [6]

A Windmill Demolishes It.

Aurora, Wise Co., Tex., April 17.—(To The News.)—About 6 o'clock this morning the early risers of Aurora were astonished at the sudden appearance of the airship which has been sailing through the country.

It was traveling due north, and much nearer the earth than ever before. Evidently some of the machinery was out of order, for it was making a speed of only ten or twelve miles an hour and gradually settling toward the earth. It sailed directly over the public square, and when it reached the north part of town collided with the tower of Judge Proctor's windmill and went to pieces with a terrific explosion, scattering debris over several acres of ground, wrecking the windmill and water tank and destroying the judge's flower garden.

The pilot of the ship is supposed to have been the only one on board, and while his remains are badly disfigured, enough of the original has been picked up to show that he was not an inhabitant of this world.

Mr. T. J. Weems, the United States signal service officer at this place and an authority on astronomy, gives it as his opinion that he was a native of the planet Mars.

Papers found on his person—evidently the record of his travels—are written in some unknown hieroglyphics, and can not be deciphered.

The ship was too badly wrecked to form any conclusion as to its construction or motive power. It was built of an unknown metal, resembling somewhat a mixture of aluminum and silver, and it must have weighed several tons.

The town is full of people to-day who are viewing the wreck and gathering specimens of the strange metal from the debris. The pilot's funeral will take place at noon to-morrow.   S. E. HAYDON.

Original newspaper article describing the incident, by S. E. Haydon, "A Windmill Demolishes It," The Dallas Morning News, April 19, 1897, p. 5.

WILLIAM G. WEBER

Rather than write about all the documented sightings from the past, I would like to fast forward to the year of 1947. This is the year of the famous Roswell, New Mexico crash, where artifacts were recovered. The artifacts were sent to Colonel Philip J. Corso, USA (Retired), and eventually to private industry for safekeeping under company trademarks. These artifacts, which contributed to today's technology, were provided to private industries to study and develop. Alien bodies recovered were flown to Wright-Patterson Air Force base. [7]

Initially, this incident was published in newspapers, but the government elected to downplay it by stating it was a weather balloon. Thus, the start of the government cover-up pattern.

July 8, 1947, issue of the Roswell Daily Record,

UFO'S – SIGHTINGS---REPORTS - COVER-UPS

Army Denial – Weather Balloon

Courtesy, Fort Worth Star-Telegram Photograph Collection, Special Collections, The University of Texas at Arlington Library

Soon after the Roswell event, there were many reports of unidentified flying objects being seen by the public. To obtain a better understanding of what was being seen and a means to disprove of the sightings, the government created a study called **Project Sign.**

Project Sign or Project Saucer was an official U.S. government study of unidentified flying objects (UFOs) undertaken by the United States Air Force (USAF) and active for most of 1948. The project was established in 1948 by Air Force

General Nathan Farragut Twining, head of the Air Technical Service Command, and was initially named Project Saucer. The goal of the project was to collect, evaluate, and distribute within the government all information relating to UFO sightings, on the premise that they might represent a national security concern. On April 27, 1949, the U.S. Air Force publicly released a paper prepared by the Intelligence Division of the Air Materiel Command at Wright-Patterson Field, Ohio. The paper stated that while some UFOs appeared to represent actual aircraft, there was not enough data to determine their origin. *Almost all cases were explained by ordinary causes,* but the report recommended a continuation of the investigation of all sightings. [8]

Josef Allen Hynek was an American astronomer, professor, and ufologist. He is perhaps best remembered for his UFO research. Hynek acted as a *scientific advisor* to UFO studies undertaken by the U.S. Air Force.

J. Allen Hynek

UFO'S – SIGHTINGS---REPORTS - COVER-UPS

Hynek was contacted to act as a scientific consultant to Project Sign. He studied UFO reports and decided whether the phenomena described therein suggested known astronomical objects.

When Project Sign hired Hynek, he was skeptical of UFO reports. *He suspected that they were made by unreliable witnesses or by persons who had misidentified man-made or natural objects. In 1948, Hynek said, "the whole subject seems utterly ridiculous,"* and described it as a fad that would soon pass.

Project Grudge was a short-lived project by the U.S. Air Force (USAF) to investigate unidentified flying objects (UFOs). Grudge succeeded Project Sign in February 1949. It was intended to alleviate public anxiety over UFOs and persuade the public that UFOs constituted nothing unusual or extraordinary. *UFO sightings were explained as balloons, conventional aircraft, planets, meteors, optical illusions, solar reflections, or even "large hailstones."* Project officials recommended that the project be reduced in scope because the very existence of Air Force official interest encouraged people to believe in UFOs and contributed to a "war hysteria" atmosphere. On December 27, 1949, the Air Force announced the project's termination. [9]

Project Blue Book was the code name for the systematic study of unidentified flying objects by the United States Air Force from March 1952 to its alleged termination on December 17, 1969. Thousands of UFO reports were collected, analyzed, and filed. As a result of the Condon Report, which concluded that the study of UFOs was unlikely to yield major scientific discoveries, and a review of the report by the National Academy of Sciences, Project Blue Book was allegedly terminated in 1969. The Air Force supplied the following summary of its investigations:

1) No UFO reported, investigated, and evaluated by the Air Force was ever an indication of a threat to our national security.
2) There was no evidence submitted to or discovered by the Air Force that sightings categorized as "unidentified" represented technological developments or principles beyond the range of modern scientific knowledge.
3) **There was no evidence indicating that sightings categorized as "unidentified" were extraterrestrial vehicles.**

By the time Project Blue Book ended, it had collected 12,618 UFO reports and concluded that most of them were *misidentifications of natural phenomena (clouds, stars, etc.) or conventional aircraft.* According to the National Reconnaissance Office, a number of the reports could be explained, even after stringent analysis. The UFO reports were archived and are available under the Freedom of Information Act, but names and other personal information of all the witnesses have been redacted.

Beginning in 1947 with Project Sign, which then became Project Grudge and finally Project Blue Book, the U.S. Air Force conducted formal studies of UFOs, a subject of considerable public and some governmental interest. Blue Book had come under increasing criticism in the 1960s. Growing numbers of critics—including U.S. politicians, newspaper writers, UFO researchers, scientists, and some of the general public—were suggesting that Blue Book *was conducting shoddy, unsupported research or perpetrating a cover-up.* The Air Force did not want to continue its studies but did not want a cessation of studies to provoke additional cover-up charges. *UFOs had become so controversial that no other government agency was willing to take on further UFO studies.* [10]

Again, it's important to note that J. Allen Hynek had acted as a scientific advisor to UFO studies undertaken by the U.S. Air Force under the three projects: Project Sign (1947–1949), Project Grudge (1949–1951), and Project Blue Book (1952–1969). His job was to discredit witness testimony related to their individual sightings and reports.

WILLIAM G. WEBER

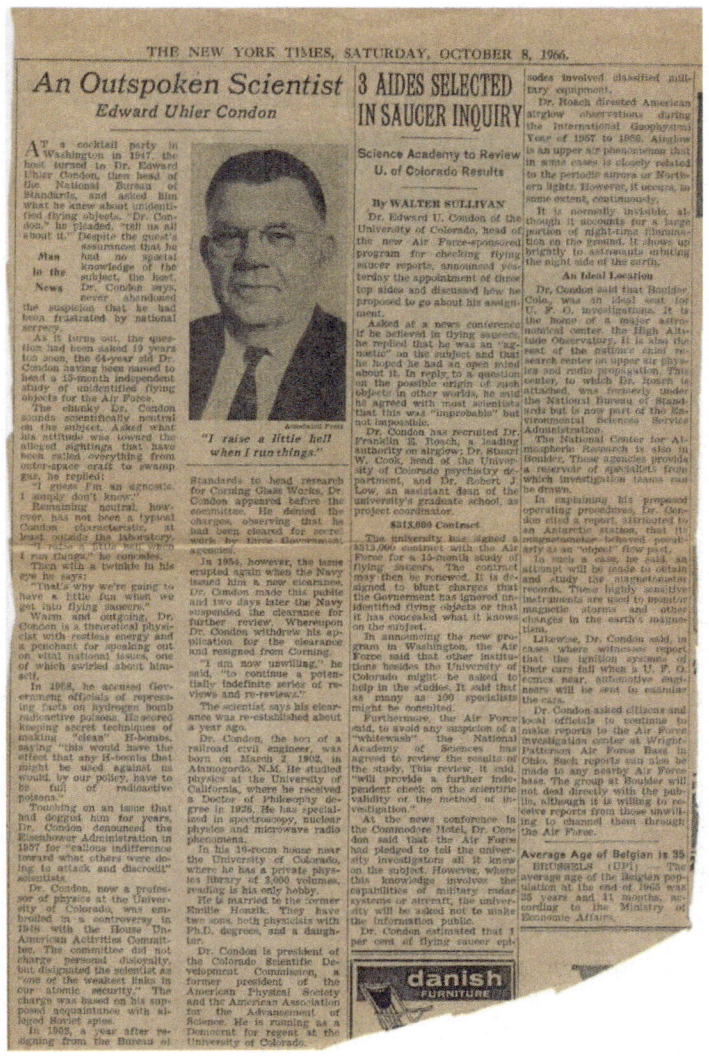

The **Condon Committee** was the informal name of the University of Colorado UFO Project, a group funded by the United States Air Force from 1966 to 1968 at the University of Colorado to study unidentified flying objects under the direction of physicist Edward Condon. The result of its work, formally titled "Scientific Study of Unidentified Flying Objects," and known as the **Condon Report**, appeared in 1968.

Edward Condon

After examining hundreds of UFO files from the Air Force's Project Blue Book and from the civilian UFO groups National Investigations Committee On Aerial Phenomena (NICAP) and Aerial Phenomena Research Organization (APRO), and investigating sightings reported during the life of the Project, the Committee produced a Final Report that said the study of UFOs was *unlikely to yield major scientific discoveries.*

The Report's conclusions received a mixed reception from scientists and academic journals. The report has been cited as a decisive factor in the generally low level of interest in UFO activity among academics since that time. According to a principal critic of the Report, it is *"the most influential public document concerning the scientific status of this UFO problem."*

As mentioned earlier, Hynek was a scientific consultant for Project Blue Book, the United States Air Force official study of the UFO phenomenon from 1948 to 1969. *Although Hynek started out as a skeptic and helped the Air Force to debunk most UFO reports,* he gradually became convinced that a small number of UFO cases were not hoaxes or explainable as misidentifications of natural phenomena and that these cases might represent something extraordinary—*even alien visitation from other planets.* When the Air Force shut down Project Blue Book in 1969, Hynek, in 1973, founded the Center for UFO Studies **(CUFOS)** to continue to collect and study UFO reports.

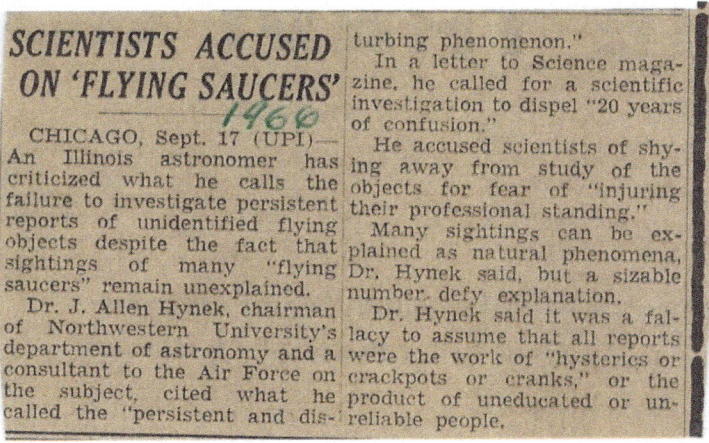

Then in 1977, at the First International UFO Congress in Chicago, Hynek presented his thoughts in his speech "What I Really Believe About UFOs." "I do believe," he said, "that the ***UFO phenomenon as a whole is real,*** but I do not mean necessarily that it's just one thing. We must ask whether the diversity of observed UFOs ... all spring from the same basic source, as do weather phenomena, which all originate in the atmosphere", or whether they differ "as a rain shower differs from a meteor, which in turn differs from a cosmic-ray shower." We must not ask, Hynek said, simply which hypothesis can explain the most facts, but rather which hypothesis can explain the most puzzling facts. Regarding hypotheses of extraterrestrial intelligence (ETI) and extradimensional intelligence (EDI), Hynek continued, **"There is sufficient evidence to defend both"**. As evidence for the ETI hypothesis, he mentioned the cases involving radar as good evidence of something solid, as well as the cases of physical evidence.

Author's Note: There is additional evidence of denials of the existence of UFOs you'll see as you read the material provided in this book. I implore you to digest the material presented and then decide for yourself if this is real or not. Today, there are organizations that are involved in understanding the UFO phenomena. They are CUFOS (Center for UFO Studies), NUFORC (National UFO Reporting Center), and MUFON (Mutual UFO Network).

CUFOS, founded in 1973, is a non-profit organization that includes scientists, professionals, academics, investigators, and others, all volunteers, dedicated to the study and analysis of the UFO phenomenon. Their purpose is to promote serious scientific interest, investigation, and research on UFOs, to serve as an archive for reports, documents, and publications about the UFO phenomenon, and to be an educational resource for the public.

NUFORC, founded in 1974, is a non-governmental, non-profit corporation registered in Washington State that documents UFO sightings and/or alien contacts. NUFORC is a trusted agency utilized by pilots, military, law enforcement, and civilians to report UFO sightings. All reports are freely available to the public.

MUFON, founded in 1969, right after the alleged shut down of Project Bluebook, is a US-based non-profit organization composed of civilian volunteers who are trained to investigate and analyze UFO sighting reports via direct contact with sighting witnesses and multiple authorities, as well as the use of a myriad of internet tools available. The sighting reports are kept in a searchable database with over one hundred thousand reports. It is one of the oldest and largest organizations of its kind, claiming more than 4,000 members worldwide with chapters and representatives in more than 43 countries and all 50 states. This book was written to examine and provide information related to several cases that have been reported, investigated, and essentially closed. Final cases disposition was determined to be unknown.

References

1) https://listverse.com/2018/03/04/10-ufo-sightings-from-very-early-history /Torch In The Sky343 BC
2) https://listverse.com/2018/03/04/10-ufo-sightings-from-very-early-history/Second Punic War Sightings 218–201 BC
3) Christopher Columbus UFO sighting in 1492 - Atlantic Ocean, - October 11, - UFO Evidence/ WaterUFO.net site
4) https://www.amusingplanet.com/2020/02/the-mysterious-sky-battle-over.html
5) UFO sighting over Basel, Switzerland in 1566 (noufors.com),
   UFO sighting over Basel, Switzerland in 1566 - Basel, Switzerland - August 7, - UFO Evidence
6) mufon.com/famous_cases/Aurora%20Texas%20Crash%20Part%201%20MUFON%20Case%20file.pdf METAL FROM CRASHED UFO? – John F. Schuessler
7) The Day After Roswell, by Col. Philip J. Corso (Ret.), with William J. Birnes, Gallery Books
8) Project Sign - Wikipedia
9) https://en.wikipedia.org/wiki/Project_Grudge#:~:text=Project%20Grudge%History
10) wikipedia.org/wiki/Condon_Committee/Background

WILLIAM G. WEBER

The Year is 1965

Exeter, New Hampshire

This was an interesting year for the things that occurred throughout the year. This was the year of alleged UFO activity which may have created a stir in our lives.

On September 3rd, there was UFO activity in a little New Hampshire town named Exeter, which is roughly 53 miles north of Boston, MA. This was a clear day, with the temperature around 47°, winds from the NW at about 2 MPH. Visibility around 30 miles.

In the early morning hours, a young man, Norman Muscarello, entered the Exeter Police Station extremely nervous and upset. He spoke with the desk person named Officer Toland. He told him of his encounter with an unknown object, which approached him while he was hitchhiking to get back to his home in Exeter. He pressed Officer Toland to have someone go out to the location to see what it was.

Officer Toland contacted another Officer named Bertrand, who was on cruise patrol. Bertrand came into the station, picked up the young man, and proceeded to head out to the location directed by the young man. When they arrived, it seemed that there wasn't anything unusual happening. Then, a large object rose from behind a tree line and started coming toward them.

They both ran and got into the patrol car, where Bertrand radioed to Toland that he had witnessed the same thing. I guess they thought they would be safe while in the patrol car. Meanwhile, another officer on patrol, an Officer Hunt, heard the communication on the radio and decided to go to where Bertrand was. As he arrived, he was joined by Muscarello and Bertrand. Soon after, the object appeared again, being witnessed by all three men. They watched as the object headed away toward the town of Hampton and the ocean. Hampton is home to Hampton Beach, a summer tourist destination. Exeter police received a call from a hysterical man in Hampton, who stated the object was heading toward him. While he was talking, the call had gotten cut off. Exeter Police then contacted both the Hampton Police and Pease Air Force Base to report the incident.

Lt. Warren Contrell from Exeter Police, having read the report at around 8:00 AM, elected to contact Pease Air Force Base to reconfirm the incident. Later that afternoon, two Officers from Pease arrived at Exeter. They were Major Thomas Griffin and Lt. Alan Brandt. They went to the sighting location and then had spent time interviewing Officer Bertrand, Hunt, and Muscarello. Upon completion of the interview, they then returned to the base with little or no comment. Contrell went on to say that there were numerous reports coming in from reliable people suggesting that there was something unusual being seen.

WILLIAM G. WEBER

Exeter News-Letter

EXETER, N.H., THURSDAY, SEPT. 9, 1965   Ten Cents fr Copy   VOL. CXXXV .. NO. 36

Unidentified Flying Objects Witnessed by Exeter Police

Exeter and Kensington were centers of speculation over the weekend following reports of the sighting in two separate places of brilliantly lighted flying objects shortly after midnight on Friday.

The UFO was first reported about 12:30 a.m. when Officer Eugene Bertrand, investigating a parked car on the Exeter-Hampton bypass, found two women in the car, apparently shocked by having been chased along Rte. 101 from Epping by a brilliantly red lighted flying object until they stopped the car. While the women told their story one of them sighted the mysterious object again low on the horizon.

Not long afterward Norman J. Muscarello, 18, of 295½ Front St. came into the police station with the startling report that he had been followed by a similar flying object as he was hitchhiking toward Exeter on Rte. 150 in Kensington. Muscarello told Officer Reginald Toland, that the large, brilliant red object appeared to make passes over him as he crouched in a ditch and also over a nearby house and field.

The object soon disappeared and Muscarello hitchhiked a ride to the police station with his story. Officer Bertrand drove Muscarello back to the place where he had first seen the object. Bertrand suggested that they walk into a field where it was last seen and there they were joined by Officer David Hunt. Suddenly the UFO rose in a blinding glow of red light from behind a clump of trees. Described as about the size of a house, it hovered silently over the nearby farm buildings, frightening animals in the barn before disappearing in the distance.

Following Officer Bertrand's report at the police station at 2:55 a.m., Officer Hunt reported at 3:30 that he had again sighted the object from the police cruiser at the junction of Rte. 85 and the Exeter bypass.

These reports were augmented at the police station by a call from an agitated man at an unidentified Hampton pay station who said he had been chased by a flying saucer. The line went dead before the call was completed and the station identified. Hampton police were notified but were unable to trace the source of the call.

Since the early reports of seeing the UFO the police during the early week have received several calls of previous sightings of mysterious flying objects which have all been referred to the Air Force for investigation. There it was indicated that there was an average of one report a night during the previous week of mysterious flying objects.

Other people in the area have said that they noticed unidentified flying objects off the coast.

It's interesting to note that NICAP (National Investigations Committee on Aerial Phenomena) had reports of low-level cases which covered a period between April 1964 through August of 1965. These cases occurred in New Mexico, Connecticut, Virginia, Washington, New York, California, Pennsylvania, Texas, Oklahoma, and Montreal, Canada.

Author's Note: *It's clear that UFO's have been appearing across the US landscape by credible witnesses with, in some cases, photographs. The denial by the Airforce and dismissal of these* *reports as nothing more than balloons, swamp gas, flocks of geese, etc. is disturbing.*

Several weeks after the Muscarello sighting, the UFO had come back to Exeter. This time, it was witnessed by a seventeen-year-old teenager named Ron Smith. He was not alone at the time of the sighting but with his aunt and mother, while driving at about eleven thirty PM. His aunt saw it first, which made him stop the car, so he could see it. He saw it as it passed over the car, stopped in mid-air reversed and passed over the car again. It passed over the car a third time and then took off. Smith, his aunt, and mother went down to the Exeter Police to report the incident.

The Pease AFB commander tried to explain the sightings during a press conference at night in the field where the object was seen. He claimed the sightings were the lights at Pease, which were turned off, and radioed the base to turn them on. No one saw anything. After this, the Air Force claimed that it was beginning a thorough investigation of the UFO. USAF Maj. Hector Quintanilla, Jr., then chief of Project Blue Book, wrote a letter to EPD, explaining that the sightings were possibly associated with USAF operations. The Pentagon issued an additional statement suggesting that the UFO might have been a misidentified star or planet.

"The Exeter incidents are one of the best regarded UFO incidents for those of us that study the subject seriously that have ever happened in America," said UFO researcher and author Peter Robbins. "The reports were made by such credible, respectable, decent people that as a rationalist, I was just drawn to it."

Over the following weeks after the event, John G. Fuller, who was doing research on this for his column in The Saturday Review magazine found that there were many credible, reliable people coming forward to tell their stories of their own recent UFO encounters.

As time went on, John Fuller had written a book entitled "Incident at Exeter: The Story of Unidentified Flying Objects Over America Today" by John G. Fuller 1966. Some of the material that speaks to the Exeter, NH event were taken from this book.

November 9, 1965 – Northeast Blackout

The northeast blackout of 1965 was a significant disruption in the supply of electricity on Tuesday, November 9, 1965. Parts of Ontario in Canada and Connecticut, Delaware, Maryland, Massachusetts, New Hampshire, New Jersey, New York, Pennsylvania, Rhode Island, and Vermont in the United States were affected. Over 30 million people and 80,000 square miles were left without electricity for up to 13 hours. [2]

Besides the loss of power, the blackout triggered sensors that placed the Mt. Weather facility (to house the president in time of nuclear attack) on red alert.

Allegedly, the cause of the failure was the setting of a protective relay on one of the transmission lines from the Sir Adam Beck Hydroelectric Power Station No. 2 in Queenston,

Ontario, near Niagara Falls. The safety relay was set to trip if other protective equipment deeper within the Ontario Hydro system failed to operate properly. On a particularly cold November evening, power demands for heating, lighting, and cooking were pushing the electrical system to near its peak capacity. Transmission lines heading into southern Ontario were heavily loaded. The safety relay had been mis-programmed, and it did what it had been asked to do, that is to disconnect under the loads it perceived. As a result, at 5:16 p.m. Eastern Time, a small variation of power originating from the Robert Moses generating plant in Lewiston, New York caused the relay to trip, disabling a main power line heading into Southern Ontario.

Instantly, the load that was flowing on the tripped line redistributed to the other lines, causing them to become overloaded. Their own protective relays, which are also designed to protect the lines from overload, tripped isolating Beck Station from all of southern Ontario. With nowhere else to go, the excess load from Beck Station was redirected east, over the interconnected lines into New York State, overloading them as well, and isolating the power generated in the Niagara region from the rest of the interconnected grid. The Beck generators, with no outlet for their power, were automatically shut down to prevent damage. The Robert Moses Niagara Power Plant continued to generate power, which supplied Niagara Mohawk Power Corporation customers in the metropolitan areas of Buffalo and Niagara Falls, New York. These areas ended up being isolated from the rest of the Northeast power grid and remained powered up. The Niagara Mohawk Western NY Huntley (Buffalo) and Dunkirk steam plants were knocked offline. Within five minutes, the power distribution system in the Northeast was in chaos as the effects of overloads and the subsequent loss of generating capacity cascaded through the network, breaking the grid into "islands". Station after station experienced load imbalances and automatically shut down. The affected power areas were the Ontario Hydro System, St Lawrence-Oswego, Upstate New York, and New England. With only limited electrical connection southwards, power to the southern states was not affected.

The only part of the Ontario Hydro System not affected was the Fort Erie area next to Buffalo, which was still powered by older 25 Hz generators. Residents in Fort Erie were able to pick up a TV broadcast from New York, where a local backup generator was being used for transmission purposes. [3]

There were also a number of reports of anomalous lights, and speculation that the blackout may have been related to UFO activity in some way.

Reporting on a subsequent sighting over the Sir Adam Beck Power Plant, a newspaper reported:

"The sighting of four strange lights over the Sir Adam Beck power plant of the Ontario Hydro Electric Power commission early today revived memories of the big power blackout that hit the northeast earlier in the week.

UFO'S – SIGHTINGS---REPORTS - COVER-UPS

"Moments before the lights flickered and failed all the way to New York City, people reported seeing a strange red ball hanging over the Beck plant. A pilot landing at Niagara Falls International Airport saw a weird object hovering 'over the Niagara Falls power station." (UFO's had also been reported in the area some six weeks prior.)"

At the end of the article, it mentions: *"After the big blackout, spokesmen for the power firms denied a strange light was spotted over the power plant on the night of Nov. 9. Since then, however, they have admitted that sightings were reported by hundreds of people."* - www.nicap.org/nyne.- Syracuse Herald-Journal 11-13-65. [4]

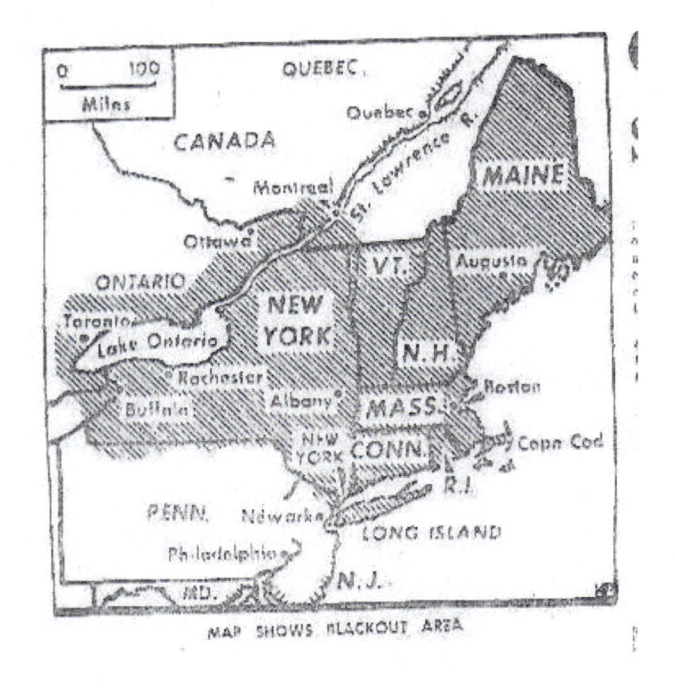

MAP SHOWS BLACKOUT AREA

WILLIAM G. WEBER

November 9, 1965

alchetron.com/Northeast–blackout–of–1965

The blackout of 1965 left about 30 million people in 80,000 square miles without power for up to 12 hours. Up to then it was the largest power failure in history and it struck at the evening rush hour. More than 800,000 riders were trapped in the city's subways.

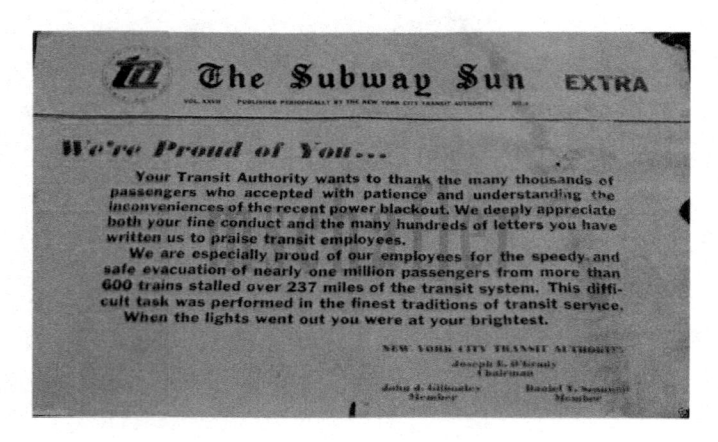

A poster placed in the New York City Subway thanking riders for staying on their best behavior during the blackout. It states "When the lights went out you were at your brightest."

Author's Note: *It is interesting to see that today, UFO's that are seen over US military installations, where there are nuclear missiles, can disable them from above, but not a simple relay...*

Western Pennsylvania

July 6, 1965; McKeesport, Pennsylvania

4:00 a.m. approximately EDT, Mrs. Hill and later her husband observed white unidentified objects in the sky. One object flew from the south towards the north and stopped at approximately an altitude of 45 degrees. Then another object came from the south and caught up with the first object and appeared to become one. Here they hovered for a minute. At this time one light flew back to the south on essentially the same path it had come while the other took off to the north. A pair of 6 X15 binoculars were used to view the objects. The teletype INCOMING MESSAGE AF IN: 5360, states: PRELIMINARY INVESTIGATION REVEALED NO OBVIOUS CONCLUSIONS OBJECT REMAINS UNIDENTIFIED. The length of the entire observation was approximately 10 minutes. [5]

August 13, 1965; Baden, Pennsylvania

9:30 p.m. - 37-year-old civilian had just put his car in the garage when he saw a disk-shaped object about 300 ft in diameter, fly in front of the moon (which rose in the E about 9:30 p.m. EDT at 107° azimuth) on a N heading at about 50 mph about 2,300 ft away, surrounded with orange lights that weakened as a blue source came on, very intense for about 3 secs. Then all lights disappeared and a sort of "shock-wave" effect shaking tree leaves ensued. The witness entered his house and called the USAF, 20 mins later his vision became hazy, eyes painful, gradually losing vision in both eyes, and his entire body was "sunburned." Medical exam compared symptoms to UV exposure. Vision came back gradually over several days. [6]

December 9, 1965 – Kecksburg, Pennsylvania

The Kecksburg UFO incident occurred on December 9, 1965, at Kecksburg, Pennsylvania, when a fireball was reported by citizens of six U.S. states and Canada over Detroit, Michigan, and Windsor, Ontario. Astronomers said it was likely to have been a meteor bolide burning up in the atmosphere and descending at a steep angle. Note: (Bolides tend to explode when entering the earth's atmosphere unlike meteors which tend to just fizzle out). NASA released a statement in 2005 reporting that experts had examined fragments from the area and determined they were from a Soviet satellite, but that records of their findings were lost in 1987. NASA responded to court orders and Freedom of Information Act requests to search for the records. The incident gained wide notoriety in popular culture and ufology, with speculation ranging from extraterrestrial craft to debris from the Soviet space probe Kosmos 96.- Space expert and skeptic James Oberg proposed the Kosmos 96 explanation in 1991 and advocated it in a 1998 Pittsburgh Post-Gazette article on the Kecksburg case.

Reports of hot metal debris over Michigan and northern Ohio, grass fires, and sonic booms in the Pittsburgh metropolitan area were attributed to the fireball. Some people in the village of Kecksburg, about 30 miles southeast of Pittsburgh, reported wisps of blue smoke, vibrations, and a "thump". They also reported that something from the sky had crashed in the woods. [7] The area where the object landed was immediately sealed off on the order of U.S. Army and State Police officials, in anticipation of a "close inspection" of whatever may have fallen. State Police officials ordered the area roped off to await the expected arrival of both U.S. Army engineers and possibly civilian scientists. Witnesses to the event indicated that they were told to leave the area by soldiers, who were carrying firearms.

Author's Note: *Interesting to see the level of security chasing folks out of the woods for just a simple meteorite, as they described the object.*

When state troopers and Air Force personnel searched the woods, they found "absolutely nothing". An AP article from December 10 stated: "State troopers and Air Force personnel tramped through the area for hours with Geiger counters. They said they found nothing and called off the search." A subsequent edition in the Tribune-Review bore the headline "Searchers Fail To Find Object".

Authorities discounted proposed explanations such as a plane crash, errant missile test, or reentering satellite debris and generally assumed it to be a meteor. Astronomer Paul Annear said the fireball was likely to have been a meteor entering the Earth's atmosphere. Geophysicist George Wetherilo discounted speculations that it was debris from a satellite and agreed that the reports were probably due to a meteor. Astronomers William P. Bidelman and Fred Hess said it undoubtedly was a meteor bolide. A spokesman for the Department of Defense in Washington said first reports indicated the reported fireball was a natural phenomenon. A UPI article from Lima, Ohio, News, dated December 11, 1965, stated: "In Washington, the Air Force said it 'concludes that the phenomenon was a meteor or meteors that entered the atmosphere.' The Air Force, which processes information on unidentified flying objects, said all aircraft and missiles were accounted for and there was no evidence of space debris which entered the atmosphere at that time."

Author's Note: *Meteors or objects falling from the sky in a straight trajectory usually do not make left-hand turns to crash in the woods. It would appear that this object was under intelligent control and slow-speed landing.*

In 2005, just ahead of the 40th anniversary of the incident, NASA announced it was a Russian satellite. But NASA couldn't prove its case because the records had been lost. "As a rule, we don't track UFOs. What we could do, and what we apparently did as experts in spacecraft in the 1960s, was to take a look at whatever it was and give our expert opinion," a NASA spokesperson said in 2005. "We did that, we boxed (the case) up and that was the end of it. Unfortunately, the documents supporting those findings were misplaced."

That wasn't NASA's line in 1965. "Investigations of photographs and sightings of the fireball indicated its path through the atmosphere was probably too steep to be consistent with a spacecraft re-entering from Earth orbit and was more likely a meteor in a prograde orbit from the vicinity of the asteroid belt, and probably ended its flight over western Lake Erie," it said in an archived press release from 1965.

NASA has steadfastly said that the Kecksburg incident was not the result of an extraterrestrial crash. "One of NASA's key goals is the search for life in the universe. To date, NASA has yet to find any credible evidence of extraterrestrial life; however, NASA is exploring the solar system and beyond to help us answer fundamental questions, including whether we are alone in the universe," NASA told Motherboard in an email. "We lead the U.S. government's search for extraterrestrial life, be it close to home, on the planets or moons of our solar system, or deeper into space. NASA does not actively search for UAPs, and the lack of robust data is the central problem for scientific study of UAPs and to determine whether they are natural or human-made phenomena—there is no current data to support that UAPs or UFOs are evidence of alien technologies." [8]

It has been alleged that the acorn-shaped object with hieroglyphics on one side was witnessed being placed on a flatbed military vehicle and transported west, eventually ending up at Wright-Patterson AFB in Dayton, Ohio.

UFO'S – SIGHTINGS --- REPORTS - COVER-UPS

The Tribune-Review
COUNTY EDITION
VOL. 80, NO. 261
GREENSBURG, PA., FRIDAY, DECEMBER 10, 1965

ARMY ROPES OFF AREA—
'Unidentified Flying Object' Falls Near Kecksburg

A model of the alleged object, created for Unsolved Mysteries, is on display near the Kecksburg fire station

Author's Note: *This incident proved to be more interesting as other investigators were involved in trying to determine what really happened here. The following is one such example of the continuing interest in the case.*

A Question — Is Case Finally Closed on 1965 Pennsylvania 'UFO Mystery'[9]

Whatever took place in Kecksburg, a dutiful look into the episode escalated to a lawsuit against NASA for access to information on the incident.

A central figure in the weirdness is New York-based investigative journalist, Leslie Kean. Working with the Coalition for Freedom of Information, it was alleged that she was on the receiving end of loads of documents as an outcome of winning the lawsuit.

This stage of the saga began in 2002 when Kean was asked to spearhead a Freedom of Information Act (FOIA) initiative sponsored by the Sci-Fi Channel in an effort to acquire government documents on the Kecksburg case. The following year, she ended up as the plaintiff in a federal FOIA lawsuit filed against NASA in Washington, DC.

After previously promising to conduct an expedited search for files related to the 1965 Kecksburg UFO crash case, NASA had stonewalled and was withholding documents, leaving no recourse but this one, Kean explained in a just-issued report. A settlement four years later, in October 2007, required NASA to provide hundreds of new documents and pay my attorney's legal fees.

NASA's resulting search, monitored by the court, was completed in August 2009. The outcome of the investigation is available in Kean's paper, which was posted online this month to the coalition's Web site.

The report flatly titled, "The Conclusion of the NASA Lawsuit - Concerning the Kecksburg, PA UFO case of 1965," explains how the process worked and the results of the search after the 2007 settlement in federal court.

The bottom line: No smoking gun documents were released, Kean notes, but many provocative questions and unresolved contradictions were raised by what was received, as well as by the fact that many files were missing or destroyed.

One open-ended aspect of Kean's reportage is the role of "Project Moondust," a U.S. government-run activity involved in examining non-U.S. space objects or objects of unknown origin. Indeed, various State Department documents show that NASA played a role in the recovery and examination of space object debris.

After months of studying the material received, Kean reports that the trail is cold, but with caveats.

"I am convinced that something came down and landed in Kecksburg," Kean told SPACE.com.

Kean thinks that a UFO connection of the extra-Earth type "is a possibility that has to be considered. It can't be ruled out," she said.

Other potentials, Kean added, "include a very secret U.S. project or another nation's hardware. But both of these explanations are unlikely."

Kean's research indicates that it appears doubtful that the object in question was either Russian or from any other country on our planet, backed up by NASA orbital debris elucidation. Also, data from the U.S. Space Command and the Russian Space Agency fortifies the fact that whatever came down that day was not a Russian satellite or space probe, she stated.

"So, I would rule that out and say it's either a UFO or a secret American device of some sort," Kean said. "If it was our own," she added, why couldn't they tell us about this 40 years later?

Therefore, that's why the UFO possibility "has to be kept in the running, as hard as it may be to accept," Kean said. "Possibly it was some kind of secretive U.S. government projects or programs for the testing of something. Maybe it was highly radioactive so they don't want anybody to know about it."

However, a central take-home message from Kean has no connection with alien visitation—more a governmental encounter of the lack-of-transparency kind.

The effort highlights the problems inherent to the use of the Freedom of Information Act in our democracy, Kean explained.

"It has been a long, long process," she said. "The important thing about this has nothing to do with UFOs. It just points out the problems with the Freedom of Information Act as it stands today."

"The NASA lawsuit was made possible because of the support of a major television network," Kean said. Also added to the investigation were John Podesta—President Clinton's former Chief of Staff—an archival research group, a lawyer, and a public relations firm in Washington, D.C.

Larry Landsman, then Director of Special Projects at the Sci-Fi Channel (now Syfy), launched the UFO advocacy initiative, with the Kecksburg lawsuit as one component of that larger undertaking. He is now an independent television producer working on various specials and miniseries.

In early 2002, a group of us began to seriously explore what initiative could be launched that would be appropriate to the spirit of the network, Landsman told SPACE.com.

"After much brainstorming, I proposed a campaign that pushed for the truth behind all of the many reports of UFOs and other unexplained phenomena. We were the first—and so far, only—company ever to pursue such an initiative and we attacked the issue on a number of fronts both on air and off air," he said.

As for Kecksburg, Landsman continued, "we felt it was a case worth investigating," supporting Kean's Freedom of Information pursuit of the full and uncensored reports about the incident.

"There were too many lives that were upended from this event and American citizens had—and have—the right to know the truth. Clearly, many things are going on in our world that cannot be easily explained," Landsman said. "Polls show that a majority of Americans believe the government is covering up information on UFOs. The truth should not be kept in the hands of only a relative few at various government agencies and military departments."

For Leslie Kean, even after years of work trying to unravel the Kecksburg incident, "what took place there is an unanswered question."

UFO'S – SIGHTINGS---REPORTS - COVER-UPS

References

1) www.abovetopsecret.com/forum/thread510798/pg1
2) Burke, James *(1985-12-17)*. *"The Trigger Effect"*. Connections. Series 1. Episode 1. Event occurs at 15:30. BBC. *Over an area of 80 million square miles, 30 million people were now in darkness.*
3) Taken from Wikipedia, Northeast Blackout of 1965
4) From NICP Report 1965 UFO Chronology – A Privatley-Supported Fact-Rinding Body Serving the Public Interest.
5) NICAP, 1965 UFO Chronology - www.nicap.org/650706mckeesport_dir
6) NICAP, 1965 UFO Chronology - www.nicap.org/650813baden_dir.
7) "Beaver County Times". news.google.com. Retrieved 2019-09-11 – via Google News Archive Search.
8) Vice.com/en/article/wx5bay/the-most-important-ufo-crash-happened-in-pennsylvania-not-roswell
9) Article copied in its entirety and written By Leonard David, published November 24, 2009- Leonard David has been reporting on the space industry for more than five decades. He is past editor-in-chief of the National Space Society's Ad Astra and Space World magazines and has written for SPACE.com since 1999.

WILLIAM G. WEBER

Carbondale, PA UFO Incident – 1974

Incident or Hoax

Carbondale, a city in Lackawanna County, Pennsylvania, United States, is located approximately 15 miles northeast of the city of Scranton in Northeastern Pennsylvania. The population was 8,828 at the 2020 census. The land area that became Carbondale was developed by William and Maurice Wurts, the founders of the Delaware and Hudson Canal Company, during the rise of the anthracite coal mining industry in the early 19th century. It was also a major terminal of the Delaware and Hudson Railroad. Carbondale was the site of the first deep vein anthracite coal mine in the United States and was the site of the Carbondale mine fire, which burned from 1946 to the early 1970s. Carbondale has struggled with the demise of the once-prominent coal mining industry that had once made the region a haven for immigrants seeking work. Immigrants from Wales, England, Scotland, Ireland, Italy, and from continental Europe came to Carbondale in the 19th and early 20th centuries to work in the anthracite and railroading industry. (Wikipedia, Carbondale, PA) Carbondale is 92.2 miles (148.4 km) north of Allentown and 130.8 miles (210.5 km) northwest of New York City.

UFO'S – SIGHTINGS---REPORTS - COVER-UPS

Prior to the Carbondale incident, there have been numerous reports of UFOs in the area. One, in particular, was reported to NUFORC on February 15, 1974. This sighting took place at Simpson, PA, which is about 2 miles from Carbondale.

Shown below is the actual witness statement that was sent to NUFORC.

NUFORC Sighting 68976

Occurred: 1974-02-15 22:10 Local - Approximate

Reported: 2009-02-27 14:48 Pacific

Duration: 10 + minutes

Number of observers: 10

Location: Simpson, PA, USA

Shape: Unknown

Characteristics: Lights on object, Left a trail

WILLIAM G. WEBER

Hovered- Colored lights went out- sped away -left trail

"This was a long time ago, but it is still fresh in my mind. I saw a red and green light over the mountain where there is a Christmas star that is turned on for the holiday. Upon driving north on route 171 in Simpson Pa, I saw the red light move over the highway.

I drove over the bridge going home and saw a number of cars on the side of the road. There were at least 10 people watching this. I stopped and got out of my car; we were all watching the lights moving over the road. The lights stopped and they hovered for about 2 minutes.

Then the red and green lights went out and a bright white appeared in the middle and sped off. It left a trail of white light behind it, because is moved so fast.

I don't know if this means anything, but it was something that I will never forget." [1]

NUFORC Note:

Source of the report indicates that the date of the incident is approximate.

The Carbondale Event: As the story goes ---- In the early evening, around 7:00 PM, on Saturday, November 9, 1974, several teenage boys; John Lloyd, age 14, William Lloyd, age 16, and Robert Gillette, age 15, were in the area of Russell Park in Carbondale PA. They reported seeing a fast-moving, brightly lit object flying across the sky. According to these witnesses, this object was moving in a westward direction coming over Salem Mountain at a very low altitude. The object then seemed to stop briefly in mid-air before crashing into a silt pond just beyond Russell Park to the South. The boys immediately began telling people what they had seen, beginning with a group of younger children nearby. Also, they reported that there was now a glowing object beneath the surface of the pond's cloudy water. At this point, other curious children and adults went to the pond to see for themselves what was happening. For sure, there was something glowing in the water. The original eyewitness story continued to be retold and circulated throughout the neighborhood. During this time period, the Carbondale Police received several calls concerning both an object falling from the sky and an unidentified glow from the pond. The Acting Chief Dottle met with Officer Trella and other officers, who first arrived on the scene around 9 pm and observed the light glowing beneath the surface of the pond. Some witnesses reported that at one-point Officer Jacobino fired his revolver into the water at the light. --*The official Police Department position on this is that no shots were fired by anyone throughout the entire incident.*

Artwork by Bruce Minney

Later, Chief Dottle contacted J. Allen Hynek (CUFOS Director), NASA, and NORAD to report the incident. Early Sunday morning as word of this unusual event continued to circulate, the numbers of onlookers were approaching greater than 2,000 people. Neighboring Wayne County Sheriff's Deputy Edwin Bailey (MUFON SSD) also went to Carbondale to investigate the several sightings being reported in the Wayne County area. He arrived sometime Sunday afternoon. Bailey wanted to dive into the pond but was refused permission by Dottle. Later that morning, the Carbondale Fire Department was summoned to the scene with a small boat, a net, and various other implements. The mysterious light had now been glowing eerily for at least seven hours, and authorities were anxious to put an end to this incident before things got stranger. With this goal in mind, Officer Trella and others went out in the boat, which was tethered to shore by a rope stretched across a section of the pond. After a short time, it appeared that they had snagged the object, which caused the pole holding a net to bend, but before they could raise it very far, it slipped out of their net, at which time the light appeared to move away from the boat. A short time later, the light grew dim and then went out completely. After Chief Dottle advised Hynek what had happened, Hynek told Dottle that he would send out a representative – Douglas Dains (MUFON Regional Director, NY). As the crowd continued to grow, Dottle elected to clear everyone out of the area, also refusing admission to the group of newsmen that was growing as well. [2]

Artwork by Bruce Minney

Sunday afternoon found the authorities still on the scene at the shoreline of the pond being joined by a rapidly growing crowd of spectators and media personnel. The rapid word-of-mouth reports of this event were now being magnified and sensationalized by local media outlets, national news wire services, and finally, national news networks. Hundreds of people were now flocking to Carbondale from all over the Northeast, including a number of ufologists, who were trying to determine if this was a legitimate UFO sighting and/or crash. Acting Chief Dottle of the Carbondale Police now had a bigger problem than what was in the pond. He had a huge and growing crowd of people wandering around an abandoned industrial area, and he had a town completely gridlocked by out-of-town traffic. Coupled with the police phone lines constantly ringing with calls from reporters, UFO "experts," and the randomly curious, it was a public safety nightmare.

To assist with crowd/traffic control, Dottle called on the Civil Air Patrol. Their arrival immediately started and spread the rumor that *"The military or Air Force was now on the scene of the UFO crash in Carbondale."* Along with this, the Police spent a considerable amount of time on the phone with officials from NORAD and NASA answering questions about the incident.

On Monday morning, the 11th, when Dains arrived, Dottle concluded that he had to put an end to this incident as quickly as possible. The first plan was to bring in a number of fire companies and have them pump the pond down to retrieve the object. A short time after the pumping operations began, it was

UFO'S – SIGHTINGS---REPORTS - COVER-UPS

determined that the silt from the pond, as well as other debris, was clogging the suction lines. A diver from Auburn, NY, Mark Stamey, who heard the reports on the radio, drove to Carbondale with his equipment offering to go into the pond to see what was down there. After some discussion, seeing no other alternative, the Acting Chief Dottle gave the diver his approval.

Driver Mark Stamey, of Syracuse, N.Y., lifts the UFO - the lantern - from the slit pond ending the mystery.

The diver first submerged near where the light was initially observed, and after a few long minutes, he resurfaced empty-handed. He then moved in the direction where the light had been seen moving after the first retrieval attempt and submerged again. This time he returned to the surface and held aloft an electric railroad lantern and handed it to the officials in a nearby rowboat. He did indeed find something in the pond that made no sense. It seemed that the incident was solved with the discovery of the railroad lantern, as declared by Dottle.

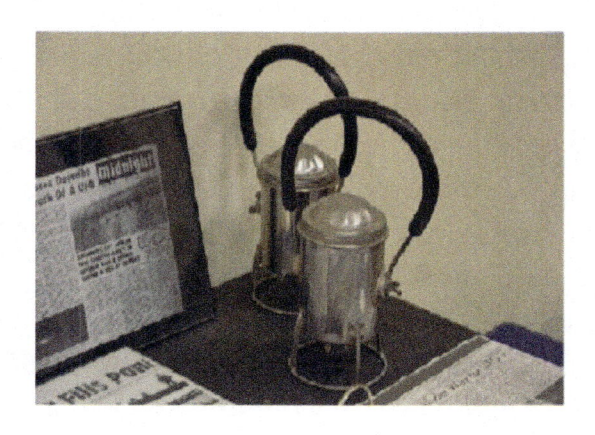

A typical Railroad Lantern – Photo courtesy Pennlive.com

However, police officer Mark Terella, who was in the rowboat, told the MUFON investigator Doug Dains at the scene that prior to the diver and lantern discovery, something was recovered using a net and pole. That object caused the pole to bend, and eventually, the object slipped out of the net that held it. Terella told Dains that this object was about 2 feet in diameter and perhaps was attached to something else that was larger. It was alleged that Doug Dains was cautioned not to say anything about this object and to stick to the lantern story by Chief Dottle. It was also interesting that Chief Dottle had denied that any shots were fired into the pond during his news conference. It seems that Dottle wanted to stick to the hoax story **period**. For days, this incident just didn't disappear, as numerous people have claimed that at some point a flatbed truck, looking like a military vehicle came in and quietly left carrying a large covered object over back roads, to who knows where. Other witnesses stated that a delivery truck from a department store was permitted past the police barricades on Sunday prior to diver Stamey's arrival and did not return. This truck could use the same route the alleged military flatbed was to take. The delivery truck would be one way of taking something away from the pond. Dottle states that he did not authorize any vehicle to enter the closed area, and his men had reported not seeing any. According to The Carbondale News, witnesses stated they saw a scuba diver in the pond on Sunday prior to diver Stamey's arrival. Could that diver be Deputy Bailey, who was also an experienced scuba diver? According to the Carbondale News, witnesses stated that there was a diver in the pond Sunday afternoon, during the period when the area was closed off to the public and press. An interesting point is that Bailey said he did dive and Chief Dottle said he didn't. What's also interesting about this case is the fact that one of the teenagers who first reported the UFO – Robert Gillette, came forward and admitted, 25 years after the fact, that they did throw the lantern in the pond as a prank to scare a group of younger kids. While this seems like a good answer to finally bring the incident to a conclusion, it seems that some who lived in or near Carbondale at the time may know someone who played some part in the potential government/police cover-up/conspiracy that took place. Was the teenager (now a man) part of the cover-up?

There is some speculation that during the time the press and the public were locked out from the site. It is thought that police officers and others could have removed something from the pond, taken it out of the area, and planted the lantern. Dottle disagrees and stated *"if we found something there, I would want the public to know what it was."* However, there was a period of over 12 hours when the public and the press were excluded from the site. *Many things can occur in 12 hours.*

On Sunday, the day before the Stamey dive, Chief Dottle ordered some heavy equipment into the area. What was needed was a crane, with a **strong magnet and grappling hooks** to come into the area.

Author's Note: *It makes you wonder why Chief Dottle was trying to suppress this incident and make it go away, or was he?*

There's more to the story.... as Mary Sutherland of BUFO (Burlington UFO Center, IL) tends to believe. She feels the lantern was planted at the sight by Chief Dottle and later found by the diver. By doing this, she felt there was a cover-up being created. Her conclusion was based on her performing a *"Remote Viewing"* or *"Psychic Photography"* session. What's interesting is the fact that she was never at the scene. She was attempting to make this a real UFO crash incident.

Author's Note: *I tried to contact Ms. Sutherland to discuss via email and telephone with no success.*

UFO'S – SIGHTINGS---REPORTS - COVER-UPS

Looking more into this, it appears to be some disagreement between two investigative entities... Mary Sutherland of BUFO and Matt Graeber, who has been interested in the UFO phenomenon and as a result, started The UFO Report and Information Center (UFORIC), based in Philadelphia.

Matt Graeber, having arrived at Carbondale at about 4:30 – 5:00 am on Monday morning, the 11th took an active part in this investigation. Along with him, a Robert Barry who was with the 20th Century UFO Bureau had come to the site as well.

Mr. Graeber stated that Mary Sutherland was on a quest to promote this as a real crash, without checking in with the witnesses and doing real research and investigation. He indicated that she had published much disinformation on her website, without any proof, documentation, evidence, or testimony. He feels that it's a shame that she is attacking the integrity and character of Detective Sergeant Francis Dottle, with her campaign of disinformation and untruths, stating that he was fabricating a hoax as a cover-up.

Earlier, Matt Graeber believed that what was witnessed was a meteorite or bolide descending from east to west, believed to have traveled out of the vision of the boys. Following the path of the meteorite, the boys assumed it went into the pond, which explained the glowing light. But at that time, he had no explanation of how the lantern got into the pool prior to the bolide sighting. How did it get there, and who placed it?

Graeber stated that his investigation proves this was a hoax and reinforces this with the fact that Robert Gillette came out 25 years later admitting to the *Scranton Sunday Times*, November 7, 1999, that he threw the lantern into the pond to scare some children. *End of story... or was it?*

Robert Barry suspected this was a cover-up as he thought the lantern story was a hoax. Allegedly, he told the Philadelphia Inquirer newspaper that he had information from "sources" that an unknown object was secretly removed by the police during the time the pond was closed to the press and public. It was then that the lantern was thrown into the pond. Later on, he stated that as far as he was concerned, in his words, *"the flashlight was a hoax."*

Another story came out regarding this event. Allegedly, Sheriff's Deputy Edwin Bailey did make a dive into the pond prior to the recovery of the lantern. The *Carbondale News* quoted witnesses that a scuba diver was in the pond on Sunday afternoon when the area was closed to the public and press. Was there a dive into the pond? Dottle says no. According to the story, Bailey had made the dive on Sunday, the 10th in the afternoon. This was prior to Mr. Dains and Mr. Graeber's arrival on Monday the 11th. Apparently, Bailey managed to obtain a boat from the National Guard that was at the scene. The interesting thing is that Graeber stated that the National Guard wasn't even there. Later on, Sunday morning – the 10th, Carbondale Fire Dept. provided a small boat (the only boat) and a net, which Trella and others used with a pole to search the pond.

Now getting back to Edwin Bailey, in a story he told the Ohio MUFON representatives, he allegedly questioned a sergeant of the National Guard where the object was to have gone into the pond. The sergeant pointed out the spot and was asked if he could provide a boat. Bailey stated that he would go out there. Shortly thereafter, the guardsman came up with a boat, which Bailey got in and went out. Apparently, he had done some tests while in the boat, using a Geiger counter to determine levels around the area. Toward the middle of the pond, he found a submerged car. Other measurements were made in an attempt to determine the depth of the pond in the target area. He came up with a figure of about 22 feet. Over time, he stated that he had found something that was about 11 feet in diameter and it was smooth. Needless to say, he did not report his findings to one of the UFO investigators on site or J. Allen Hynek. Also, why didn't he come back to the site after the crowd, the newspaper men, and the photographers left to explore further what he found? Well, his story did make the **Ohio Sky Watcher** newsletter as was told by the UFO researchers. Months later, in an interview by Jim Payson of Men magazine, which appeared in August 1975, Bailey stated that "this is not a closed book, it can't be a closed book." "We're investigating incidents relating to the same time period and same direction of travel. A real serious investigation is going on. The Carbondale incident is at present only indirectly involved in the investigation, but it may become directly involved as more material develops."

On Monday, Mark Stamey (the diver) arrived after having heard the incident report on the radio. He was given the approval by Dottle to make the dive. Officer Trella and a photographer took him to the location where they had worked with the net. Newsmen and others were allowed to watch from the area around the pond. Photographers were also present on the shore. The majority of the crowd, which was about 2,000 people, were kept outside the roped area. Stamey entered the water at 2:26 PM, searching the area shown to him. He had found nothing. Continuing his search, he found the lantern about 20 feet east of where he began. He handed it to photographer Jerome Gillott in the boat. The lamp was dimly lit and eventually, the light went out.

The lantern was shown to the crowd, and it was announced that this was what caused all the uproar. At that time, the crowd was told this was a hoax. Later in the day, Chief Dottle had a press conference at City Hall, where Mayor A.J. Kaufman reconfirmed the finding. No one offered any explanation of how the lantern ended up in the pond. Case closed – or is it?

In his report to J. Allen Hynek, Bains had implied that he was accepting the hoax theory. *"When talking to the Lloyd brothers, I had the distinct impression that they were extremely exaggerating their stories. I, therefore, find no scientific benefit for continuing this investigation. I, therefore, terminate my investigation until such time that evidence is presented to reopen the case."* The reporter Jim Payson received a copy of this report for publication in the magazine.

UFO'S – SIGHTINGS---REPORTS - COVER-UPS

Not only were the teenage boys seeing unknowns in the sky, coincidentally, two reports had come into NUFORC years later speaking of sightings around the same time.

See actual reports below:

NUFORC Sighting 10131

Occurred: 1974-01-09 21:00 Local - Approximate

Reported: 1999-10-06 00:00 Pacific

Duration: three days No of observers: 5

Location: Carbondale, PA, USA

Shape: Circle

Characteristics: Aura or haze around object, Left a trail, Landed

A circular object flew across the sky and fell into a pond. The water was bubbling and a strange blue/green color. Police and military personnel were notified. Divers went into the water and retrieved something, which was put into a large closed trailer. The official report said it was a "miner's lantern". Paul Bunyon must have thrown it from Phila. My father and I watched the whole thing. Dad died in 1976, and I have never told anyone that we watched everything that was done from a nearby hill. Neither the police nor the military knew we were watching. They had cordoned off the area so sightseers could not get near their operations. We had a bird's-eye view. (3)

Author's Note: The Carbondale event took place on the days of November 9th – 11th. This report states the event happened January 9th. Makes you wonder if this is a bogus report.

NUFORC Sighting 176040 Occurred: 1974-11-09 18:00 Local Reported: 2023-06-04 09:59 Pacific Duration: It was Nov.9, 1974 20 sec No of observers: 4

Location: Carbondale, PA, USA Location details: We were on old route 6 traveling north from Peckville to Eynon

Shape: Fireball Characteristics: Left a trail

We were traveling north on old route 6 off to our right (east) an object like a shooting star went past us.

As my wife and 2 friends were traveling north on old route 6 on Nov. 9, 1974, at 6 pm coming down the hill from Peckville to Eynon off to our right (east), a flying object resembling a shooting star flew past us. The object was silver in color with the nose in flames with blackened streaks and sparks with smoke trailing it. It was approx. 3000 ft. high and traveling south to north and located approx. the center of the Lackawanna valley. I can still vividly remember what it looked like. The government report of what they found was a complete lie. I know because we knew nothing about a UFO reported in Carbondale until a few

UFO'S – SIGHTINGS---REPORTS - COVER-UPS

days later and the story the government put to the public had to be a lie. 3 of the witnesses are still alive today. [4]

Years later, the city of Carbondale wanted to remember the event, which put a national focus on the town. As a result, they had held a party/festival after a certain milestone: the 40th anniversary of the event.

Inside the **Best Western Pioneer Plaza** in Carbondale, there was an extra special, extraterrestrial party where some dressed up for the occasion. "This was an impulse, this was to keep the lore going and a little humor," said Buckie Hosie of Carbondale. The celebration was for the 40th anniversary of a reported UFO sighting in Carbondale. In 1974, there was a report of a glowing unidentified object falling into a pond in the area. **Newswatch 16** spoke with one man who said his friend was among those at the scene 40 years ago.

"I never saw anything, but we would sit there for hours looking for UFOs allegedly happening here or sighting there but he took place in this particular extravaganza and I came down here to see if his name was listed anywhere there. He stayed all night down there; I wasn't with him. I went home, but he stayed," explained Anthony Catanzaro. Some at the party were silly about it all. "How do I like Carbondale? I love the coal, I love the people. I love myself," joked one man dressed like an alien. Others said they believe the story. "Something significant happened in Carbondale. Eighty percent of the population that were over the age of 55 and here in Carbondale at the time, 40 years ago, they're not buying the official story," said Ron

Hannivig of Fell Township. Whether they were believers or not, folks we found partying said it was a great community event. "I think it's a great event for the town just to bring the community together and enjoy some food and some fun and I think it's about time Carbondale has a great reputation and I think this party's gonna do it," said Rebecca Landmesser of Hallstead.

The Carbondale Grand Hotel (now the Anthracite Hotel) had its own planned program for the event.

They had several speakers presenting. One of the speakers was Dr. Robert Powell of the Carbondale Historical Society. Members of the Mutual UFO Network were also invited to present. The members were myself – Chief Investigator for PA, John Ventre – PA State Director, and Fred Saluga – WVA State Director. We presented information on who MUFON was as well as several reported cases to the audience. All speakers were well received.

The Times-Tribune

Carbondale UFO tale rises again

November 13, 2016

CARBONDALE, Pa. (AP) — David Morris wants to believe. The Greenfield Twp. resident was only 6 years old on Nov. 9, 1974, when then-14-year-old Robert Gillette Jr. and two friends reported to police they saw a red, whirring ball fly over Salem Mountain and followed it to a silt pond in Carbondale. At age 48, he still is intrigued by the local legend. Morris was one of dozens of people who took a county transit system trolley from Carbondale Grand Hotel to the old mine pond on Saturday to satisfy their curiosity — part of a hotel-hosted event commemorating an incident that became international news at the time. "I was curious to see if it was physically possible for something like that to have taken place," Morris said. "I think it was definitely physically possible." The "Carbondale UFO" drew police, military, UFO enthusiasts, and spectators from all over the country in 1974. A green-tinged glow illuminated the pond for nine hours; after two days, a diver emerged from the murky waters with only an old railroad lantern. Kay Pope, who was 15 at the time and is now 58, remembers riding her bicycle to the Russell Park area and seeing it cordoned off by the military. She also saw what appeared to be something large being removed from the area. "We always rode our bikes up there," said Pope, who now lives in Blakely. "(I saw) a big flatbed truck on the road with something huge on it that was covered, and there were a lot of people in (military) uniforms." Gillette told The Times-Tribune in 1999 that he threw the battery-powered, sealed-beam lantern into the water to scare his sister — but the legend has since lived on. After seeing the pond and talking with locals who were around at the time, Morris didn't buy the story that a lantern was behind it all. He was disappointed Gillette did not speak at the event because he wanted to clarify some of the details. "Why would you call in the people that were called in and heavy machinery to take a lantern out of a pond?" he wondered. "It just doesn't make any sense. I think something definitely happened there." Now 56 years old, Gillette was hanging around the hotel during Saturday's *"alien landing* anniversary and celebration" and now claims what he told the newspaper 17 years ago wasn't true. "My girlfriend broke up with me, so I was in a bad mood," he said. "I just told them what they wanted to hear, that it was a lantern. It wasn't a lantern. Something was pulled out of the pond."

Saturday's event included speakers from the Mutual UFO Network and others with expertise on the topic.

Bill Weber, the network's Chief Investigator for Pennsylvania and Delaware, said in an interview that at this time, he doesn't have extensive knowledge about the Carbondale incident, and based on what he knew, *"I think the jury is still out." "I hear reports of lights in the sky, maneuvers in the sky, unknown objects, triangles in the sky,"* Weber said. *"In Pennsylvania, we average about 25 to 35 cases a month. We have means of testing the credibility. ... We take the report, we establish contact with the witness or witnesses, and we do our investigation, internet searches, FAA requests, local police, state police requests. We try to get to the bottom of it."* In 85 percent of the cases, investigators are able to explain what people saw, he estimated. The other 15 percent of the time, they are not.

For his part, Gillette did not think aliens were responsible for what he saw, but perhaps a Soviet satellite. "I don't think it was aliens. Some people do," the city resident said. "I never called it a UFO. The official people did." Richard Suraci, a marketing and

UFO'S – SIGHTINGS---REPORTS - COVER-UPS

sales official for Carbondale Grand Hotel, envisions the festivities becoming an annual event to celebrate an interesting piece of the city's history.

To remember the event, the city of Carbondale put up a historical monument at McCawley Park.

McCawley Park: Carbondale's UFO Marker Photographed by William Fischer Jr., June 7, 2019

References

1) THE Carbondale UFO Crash, 11-11-1974 (ufocasebook.com)
2) UFO Crash Cases (ufocasebook.com)
3) Payson, Jim. (1975, August). Pennsylvania's Mysterious UFO "Lantern." Men, 28–30, 74-79.
4) Magonia Supplement No 55 2005 03 15: Free Download, Borrow, and Streaming : Internet Archive
5) The Carbondale Chronicles by Matt Graeber (roswellfiles.com)
6) UFOs at close sight: home page. (patrickgross.org)
7) Carbondale UFO Crash, Reality, hoaxes and the legend by M.J. Graeber
8) The artwork was by Bruce Minney
9) CARBONDALE UFO CRASH CHRONICLES No.10- Case Closed – by Matt Graeber,   edited by Scott Elliott
10) nuforc.org/sighting/?id=68976, NUFORC02/15/1974,Simpson,PA,USA,- Unknown-Hovered-Colored lights-went out-sped away-left trail
11) The Carbondale UFO Crash Chronicles, entries 2 through 10. UFO Updates archives
12) Posted 1999-10-19- NUFORC Reports for State PA
13) Posted 2023-07-10 - updb.app/report/2-S176040

UFO'S – SIGHTINGS---REPORTS - COVER-UPS

Incident at Joint Base McGuire/Dix/Lakehurst

January 18, 1978

The true story of an event which occurred at Joint Base McGuire/Dix/Lakehurst as told to me and written by myself and Major George Filer (retired) on April 26, 2023

Joint Base McGuire/Dix/Lakehurst is a United States military facility located 18 miles southeast of Trenton, New Jersey. The base is the only tri-service base in the United States Department of Defense and includes units from all six-armed forces branches. The facility is an amalgamation of the United States

Air Force's McGuire Air Force Base, the United States Army's Fort Dix, and the United States Navy's Naval Air Engineering Station Lakehurst, which were merged on October 1st, 2009.

McGuire hosts the U.S. Air Force 21st Air Force Military Airlift Command now called Air Mobility Command. *"The 21st was in charge of the Air Force aircraft in half the world, from the Mississippi River east to India, including air bases and posts in Europe and the Atlantic Ocean,"* The reach included 10 bases with about 600 aircraft. McGuire had 60-80 aircraft, including three squadrons of C-141s. Each squadron had 23 aircraft. All of this was under a single wing commander, who ran the 21st Expeditionary Mobility Task Force command center.

Fort Dix has a history of mobilizing, training, and demobilizing soldiers from as early as World War 1 through the present day. In 1978, the first female recruits entered basic training at Fort Dix. In 1991, Dix trained Kuwaiti civilians in basic military skills so they could take part in their country's liberation. Fort Dix ended its active Army training mission in 1988 due to Base Realignment and Closure Commission recommendations. It began a new mission of mobilizing, deploying, and demobilizing soldiers and providing training areas for Army Reserve and Army National Guard soldiers.

The Navy's lighter-than-air program was conducted at Lakehurst through the 1930s. It was the site of the 1937 LZ 129 Hindenburg airship disaster. During World War II, anti-submarine patrol blimps were operated from Lakehurst. Since the 1950s, Aviation Boatswain's Mates have been trained at

UFO'S – SIGHTINGS---REPORTS - COVER-UPS

Lakehurst to operate catapults and arresting systems on aircraft carriers. Lakehurst conducts the unique mission of supporting and developing the Aircraft Launch and Recovery Equipment and Support Equipment for naval aviation.

I have to admit, over my many years of researching and investigating UFO events, I found this one particularly interesting and have decided to do my own digging into the fascinating incident. No longer being with MUFON (Mutual UFO Network), I have more time available to give this subject the attention that it deserves.

So, some of the details about this case, which were reported by multiple sources, reveal some ambiguities from one source to another. As a result, I decided to start by connecting with Major George Filer III, USAF (Retired), who was the Deputy Director, 21st Airforce Intelligence. At the time of the event, he was stationed at McGuire AFB, where the incident took place.

I had the opportunity to meet and interview Major Filer at his home in Medford, NJ on April 26, 2023, at approximately 11:20 AM. Major Filer has had an interesting career in the USAF that has spanned over 20 years.

He is no stranger to UFOs, as he had shared several of his experiences with me. One of which is as follows:

"When flying for the 420th Air Refueling Squadron from Sculthorpe RAF Base, England in February of 1962, we were in orbit for USAF refueling operations over the North Sea at 30,000 feet in our six-engine KB-50 J tanker aircraft.

Photo of KB-50J aircraft.

At about 7:00 PM, London Control excitedly notified us that they had an unidentified object hovering between Oxford and Stonehenge at around 1,000 feet altitude. We were asked if we were willing to investigate. Our refueling mission was about over, so we quickly agreed to chase their UFO. We were given an intercept heading and started to dive toward the UFO. This was really fun and exciting compared to a standard mission. I never could recall such speed and power as our six engines were advanced to full military power as we dove on the target.

London Control was diverting commercial aircraft to clear our path for the intercept in what they called the same as the "Queens Clearance" down to Stonehenge. We started descending and picking up speed. The plane started vibrating, and I realized we were above our red line maximum speed, slowing the jet engines and had trouble reducing the speed of our aircraft. London Control started giving our distance to the hovering UFO. They called out your 100 miles apart, 60, and 40. At about 30 miles my APS-23 Radar seems to pick up the hovering UFO directly ahead. It was an exceptionally large radar return reminding me of a large Forth of Forth bridge or a large passenger ship. This craft was as big or bigger than anything I had seen in the air before. The UFO appeared to be a Cylinder.

Firth of Forth railroad bridge, Scotland

The return was sharp and solid as compared to the fuzziness of rain clouds. I felt this craft must be made of steel or strong metal. We were doing around 425 mph as we approached about ten miles when it apparently realized we were intercepting. It was a dark night; we could only see a series of dim lights directly ahead and a long cylinder. Now only five miles separated us. Suddenly the UFO seemed to come alive, the lights brightened, and the UFO accelerated in a launch similar to the Space Shuttle at night. We saw much brighter lights and fantastic acceleration almost straight up, and suddenly it was gone.

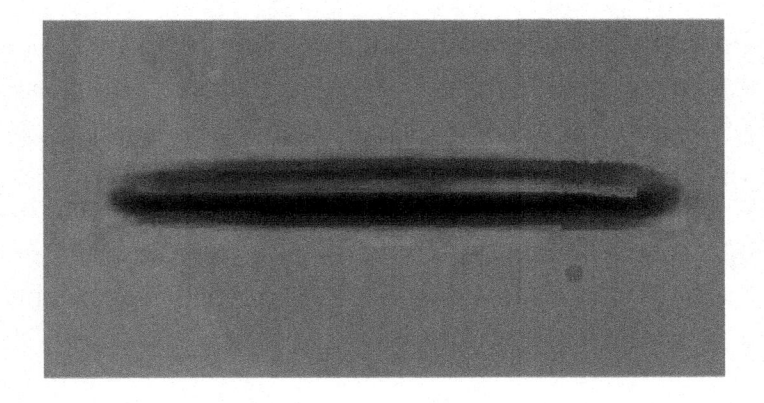

Image of UFO

We asked London Control, "If they had any rocket launches in the area?" London Control seemed as disappointed as we were. The controller said, "There are no rocket launches in that area, thank you for the intercept, you are now cleared to return to your mission." Our mission was no longer a priority, and we had to fly the normal routine traffic patterns. It is clear they felt there was a strong return for the 20 to 25 minutes it had taken to reach the UFO. We had been cleared directly through various altitudes, airways, and commercial traffic, so they must have considered this mission very important. I can still see that return in my mind's eye, and I've been chasing UFOs ever since.

UFO'S – SIGHTINGS---REPORTS - COVER-UPS

The event was reported; however, nothing was said about it. The USAF was silent on the subject as well."

George Filer stated: "When I chased a UFO over England when flying for the US Air Force, I've been investigating them ever since. My experience was as an intelligence officer who briefed generals, was a master navigator, occasional co-pilot, flight planner for President Ford and Carter and Secretary of State Henry Kissinger, aerospace science instructor, and later Vice President of Medcor, Inc."

During that weekend, Prince Philip (the Queen's husband) was to give a casual speech at the Officers club, where there were about 100 officers dining in.

Prince Phillip

After the speech, Prince Philip mentioned the particular event and wanted to meet with the crew of the KB-50J aircraft to discuss it. Prince Philip had an interest in the subject of UFOs, which was sparked by stories told by his uncle – Lord Mountbatten, who was a UFO enthusiast. It seems that Lord Mountbatten had his own experiences when an unknown craft was hovering on his estate in February of 1955.

Lord Mountbatten had made an official report about a strange encounter his bricklayer Fred Briggs allegedly had with a flying saucer and an alien creature. The article was published by the Sun and is shown below:

From an article written by Emma Parry, Published: 12:41, 25 Sep 2017, and Updated: 13:14, 25 Sep 2017, which appeared in a British tabloid newspaper called the Sun, which is published by the News Group Newspapers division of News UK, itself a wholly-owned subsidiary of Rupert Murdoch's News Corp.

"PRINCE Philip's uncle Lord Mountbatten was a UFO enthusiast and even wrote an official report about an alien in a silver spaceship landing on his estate, historical documents show.

Mountbatten was a 'hugely important and influential Ufologist' even though he kept his interest in the paranormal a secret throughout his life," according to UFO expert Alejandro Rojas. Back in February of 1955, Mountbatten, who was often referred to as Prince Charles's "honorary godfather" and mentor because of his close relationship with the Duke of Edinburgh, made an official

UFO'S – SIGHTINGS --- REPORTS - COVER-UPS

report about a strange encounter his bricklayer Fred Briggs allegedly had with a flying saucer and an alien creature.

The report, which was uncovered after Mountbatten's 1979 death at the hands of the IRA, describes how a silver spaceship landed in the grounds of his Broadlands estate in Romsey, Hampshire. The flying saucer hovered above the ground before a man dressed in overalls and a helmet descended from the bottom of the craft, according to the documents. Fred was then reportedly knocked off his bike and held on the ground by an 'unseen force'.

Statement by Frederick S. Briggs, 8, Chambers Avenue, Romsey, Hants.

I am at present employed at Broadlands as a bricklayer and was cycling to my work from Romsey on the morning of Wednesday, the 23rd February 1955. When I was about half way between the Palmerston or Romsey Lodge and the house, just by where the drive forks off to the Middlebridge Lodge, I suddenly saw an object hovering stationary over the field between the end of the gardens and Middlebridge drive, and just on the house side of the little stream.

The object was shaped like a child's huge humming-top and half way between 20ft. or 30ft. in diameter.

Its colour was like dull aluminium, rather like a kitchen saucepan. It was shaped like the sketch which I have endeavoured to make, and had portholes all round the middle, rather like a steamer has.

The time was just after 8.30 a.m. with an overcast sky and light snow on the ground.

I turned off the drive at the fork and rode over the grass for rather less than 100 yards. I then dismounted, and holding my bicycle in my right hand, watched.

While I was watching a column, about the thickness of a man, descended from the centre of the Saucer and I suddenly noticed on it, what appeared to be a man, presumably standing on a small platform onthe end. He did not appear to be holding on to anything. He seemed to be dressed in a dark suit of overalls, and was wearing a close fitting hat or helmet.

At the time the Saucer was certainly less than 100 yards from me, and not more than 60ft. over the level where I was standing, although the meadow has a steep bank at this point, so that the Saucer would have been about 80ft. over the lower level of the meadow.

As I stood there watching, I suddenly saw a curious light come on in one of the portholes. It was a bluish light, rather like a mercury vapour light. Although it was quite bright, it did not appear to be directed straight at me, nor did it dazzle me, but simultaneously with the light coming on I suddenly seemed to be pushed over, and I fell down in the snow with my bicycle on top of me. What is more, I could not get up again. Although the bicycle only weighs a few lbs. it seemed as though an unseen force was holding me down.

Whilst lying on the ground I could see the tube withdrawn quickly into the Saucer, which then rose vertically, quite as fast as the fastest jet aircraft I have seen, or faster.

There had been no noise whatever until the Saucer started to move, and even then the noise was no louder than that of an ordinary small rocket let off by a child on Guy Fawkes Night.

It disappeared out of sight into the clouds almost instantaneously, and as it went, I found myself able to get up. Although I seemed to be lying a long time on the ground I do not suppose, in reality, it was more than a few seconds.

Following statement by Fred Briggs about the reported landing of a UFO on Lord Mountbatten's estate in 1955 - Credit: Broadlands Archives

"The object was shaped like a child's huge humming-top and halfway between 20ft or 30ft in diameter," the official report states.

"Its color was like dull aluminum, rather like a kitchen saucepan. It was shaped like the sketch which I have endeavored to make, and had portholes all around the middle, rather like a steamer has."

It went on: "While I was watching, a column, about the thickness of a man, descended from the center of the saucer and I suddenly noticed on it, what appeared to be a man, presumably standing on a small platform on the end."

"He did not appear to be holding on to anything. He seemed to be dressed in a dark suit of overalls and was wearing a close-fitting hat or helmet."

UFO'S – SIGHTINGS---REPORTS - COVER-UPS

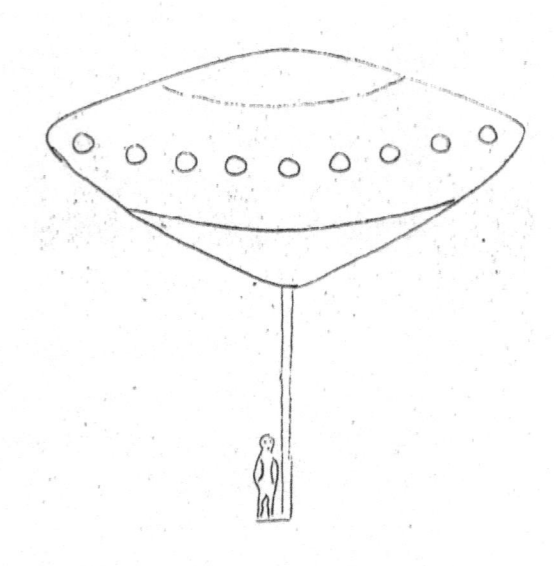

A sketch of the UFO and alien reported on Mountbatten's estate – Credit: Broadlands Archive

Fred added: *"As I stood there watching I suddenly saw a curious light come on in one of the portholes. "It was a bluish light rather like a mercury vapor light." "Although it was quite bright, it did not appear to be directed straight at me, nor did it dazzle me, but simultaneously with the light coming on I suddenly seemed to be pushed over and I fell down in the snow with my bicycle on top of me. What is more, I could not get up as though an unseen force was holding me down."* The flying saucer then disappeared out of sight *"almost instantaneously"*

WILLIAM G. WEBER

(BROADLANDS ARCHIVES)

The attached statement was dictated by Mr. Briggs to Mrs. Travis on the morning of the 23rd February 1955 at my request.

My own electrician, Heath, reported his conversation and I subsequently interviewed Mr. Briggs, with my wife and younger daughter, and as a result of his account, Heath and I accompanied him to the place from which he saw the Flying Saucer.

We followed the marks of his bicycle in the snow very easily, and exactly at the spot which he described the tracks came to an end, and foot marks appeared beside it. Next to the foot marks there were the marks of a body having fallen in the snow, and then the marks of a bicycle having been picked up again, there being a clear gap of 3ft. between where the front wheel marks originally ended and then started again. The rear wheel marks were continuous but blurred. From then on the bicycle tracks led back to the drive.

The bicycle tracks absolutely confirm Mr. Briggs' story, so far as his own movements are concerned.

He, Heath and I searched the area over the spot where the Flying Saucer was estimated to have been, but candidly we could see no unusual signs.

The snow at the bottom of the meadow had melted much more than that at the top, and it would have been difficult to see any marks.

This statement has been dictated in the presence of Heath and Mr. Briggs, and Heath and I have carefully read Mr. Briggs' statement, and we both attest that this is the exact story which he told us.

Mr. Briggs was still dazed when I first saw him, and was worried that no one would believe his story. Indeed, he made a point of saying that he had never believed in Flying Saucer stories before, and had been absolutely amazed at what he had seen.

He did not give me the impression of being the sort of man who would be subject to hallucinations, or would in any way invent such a story. I am sure from the sincere way he gave his account that he, himself, is completely convinced of the truth of his own statement.

He has offered to swear to the truth of this statement on oath on the Bible if needed, but I saw no point in asking him to do this.

[signature: Mountbatten of Burma]

I confirm that I have read and agree with the above statement.

[signature: R.K. Heath]

Signed statement by Lord Mountbatten, describing the UFO sighting. Credit: Broadlands Archives

Mountbatten went to investigate as soon as he heard the tale - and said that Fred's bike tracks left in the snow confirmed his movements. In a signed statement, Mountbatten said: *"Mr. Briggs was still dazed when I first saw him and was worried that no one would believe his story."*

"Indeed, he made a point of saying that he had never believed in Flying Saucer stories before and had been absolutely amazed at what he had seen."

"He did not give me the impression of being the sort of man who would be subject to hallucinations or would in any way invent such a story."

"I am sure from the sincere way he gave his account that he, himself, is completely convinced of the truth of his own statement".

Ufologist Alejandro, who runs UFO site Open Minds TV, recounted the tale at the Devil's Tower UFO Rendezvous in Hulett, Wyoming. He told Sun Online that Mountbatten was "instrumental" in developing the field of UFO investigations both in the UK and around the world. "I think this story is incredibly important," he said.

"The Royals have had a history of being interested in the paranormal but Mountbatten was very interested in UFOs and he was instrumental in the UFO subject being taken more seriously and popularized in the UK. "Prior to some of the more credible books about UFOs being serialized in the UK, British people thought Americans were silly in their attention to UFOs".

Behind the scenes – and people didn't know at the time – Mountbatten was contacting different newspapers and trying to get them interested in serializing these UFO books. "He then asked them not to tell anyone that it was him who had got them to do it". They respected his request and didn't let people know. That's what makes him so important to ufology – he got people interested in this subject. Another reason is that ufology got taken over by the UK in that official UFO investigations went all the way until 2008 whereas in the United States we stopped officially investigating them in 1969. "There's a longer history of UFO investigation in the UK and that's a lot to do with Mountbatten."

"He was instrumental in making the investigation of UFOs more credible. But he kept his interest in UFOs secret while he was alive, and it wasn't known about until after his death. Prince Philip also took an interest in ufology. He was very close to his uncle and always said he was more of a father to him. 'He definitely picked up the interest in UFOs – but we are not sure if Charles and the rest of the family did – although we can tell from their reading lists that they do request different paranormal books."

Major Filer went on to share his story with the Prince. George then told me, "That on the ground in the location of Stonehenge, there is an imprint of the craft in the ground about a mile long and about 6 feet deep, shaped like a V, and the V is in the shape of the UFO again, which is about a mile long." George stated that you can look it up on the internet. He said it's called a cursus and believes that archaeologists thought it was made for horse racing long ago. George thinks the area, in the shape of a UFO was prepared over 3 - 4 thousand years ago as a nice level place for the UFO to land.

George stated that the Prince was very interested in his story. George asked why he was interested in the subject of UFOs. George stated the Prince said he had chased UFOs himself as a pilot and attempted to debrief aircrews that chase UFOs. I asked how he became interested. He said, "Lord and Admiral Mountbatten had raised him, and he was the Commander of the Navy, which had a fleet of ships in the Mediterranean Sea, they had been buzzed by UFOs and as the last Viceroy to India had seen them. He convinced me that UFOs were an important force on Earth." George went on to say that "there was no doubt in Prince Philip's mind that these things were real".

Now, getting back to this incident, needless to say, this is a very interesting topic to discuss. The Joint Base McGuire / Dix / Lakehurst incident occurred early on Wednesday, January 18, 1978. The weather that day was about 37°F, sky was cloudy, the wind was 20 mph NNE with visibility at 10 miles.

Weatherunderground/history

Following is the report and testimony of the event that Major Filer had put together in his words and given to me, so that it would be included in this chapter. It gives details of the January 18, 1978 event.

Written Report obtained from Major George Filer (Major USAF, retired) in his words

WILLIAM G. WEBER

The purpose of this research is to validate the story that an alien was shot on Wednesday, January 18, 1978, at Fort Dix, New Jersey. An Army Military Police officer, John Samuels is believed to have fired his .45 caliber pistol at an alien and his hovering craft. The alien fled to McGuire Air Force Base where he died from his wounds. The alien was put under guard and later flown to Wright Patterson AFB. The State Police were aware of the incident but were denied entrance to McGuire. Richard Hall, Bill Hall, Bruce Maccabee, and Len Stringfield interviewed the primary witness, Jim Mc Caughan. He was an Air Force Security Policeman, who had guarded the body. All agreed he was a credible witness. Richard was attempting to contact Jim and arrange for another interview. Jim claims the incident remains a closely held secret. We're building a network of investigators with Tom Carey, Richard Hall, Walt Webb, Eric Mintel, my UFO class students, and several NJ MUFON members to find additional witnesses. This case has the unique potential for determining the entire UFO phenomenon.

UFO'S – SIGHTINGS---REPORTS - COVER-UPS

LEN STRINGFIELD

Leonard Stringfield, a noted Ufologist, was director of Civilian Research, Interplanetary Flying Objects (CRIFO), and published a monthly newsletter, ORBIT. In 1957 he became public relations adviser for the civilian UFO group, National Investigations Committee On Aerial Phenomena (NICAP), under the direction of Donald Keyhoe, a friend since 1953. From 1967 to 1969, Stringfield served as an "Early Warning Coordinator" for the Condon Committee. During the 1970s, he wrote a number of books about alleged crash recoveries of alien spaceships and alien bodies.

During the last several years prior to Len Stringfield's death I talked to him numerous times about the case. Shortly before his death, Len told me McGuire may be potentially his most important case because of the government's continued denial of the Roswell, New Mexico crash. In reviewing my notes from our conversations during the fall of 1994, I came across some important information. Len claimed he had talked with a Major who was the pilot of the C-141 that carried the body back to Wright Patterson. The Major knew there was an alien body. I believe he was in the C-141 Test Squadron at Wright Patterson. I particularly wanted to talk to him since I had flown the C-141s.

Len said, *"He had no updates from Jim Mc Caughan, since the McGuire Security Policeman, left the country. Jim was going back first to Korea and then was taking a job in the Philippines. Jim was very frightened and indicated that this would likely be the last time you'll see me."*

Len had another source whose principal work in the Air Force was with crash recovery. He now lives near Cincinnati. Len talked to his daughter because direct contact was so dangerous. The daughter said, *"Dad had one phone number where he could be reached. No one knew his destination; he would travel to crash retrievals all around the world. He was called in the middle of the night in January of 1978 and told to immediately go to McGuire Air Force Base. He was sent to a little town called Wrightstown next to the base and brought his family to stay with him. They stayed for two weeks, but his family was not allowed to go on the base. It was all secret stuff; he was not allowed to tell his family anything. The family stayed in a motel in Wrightstown, and he stayed on the base. They didn't see him for about two weeks because he was so tied up with whatever was going on. Dad later told us that the reason he was gone had involved an alien craft. Dad said, "I want to tell you a story; there were a number of objects flying in the area that were picked up on radar. One of the craft became disabled; he did not say crash, but disabled. This caused the occupants to be scattered around, one happened to stray into a military area, possibly near the outer road. He was challenged by a guard and didn't give the right password. The guard was trigger-happy and shot the alien. The alien lived for a while, climbed the fence, and got onto the airstrip where he died."*

Len felt the alien could have been involved in the crash of his craft or just ejected from a pod or cockpit of the UFO. Another report speculated the alien became separated from his craft and was hungry. Unfortunately, Len passed away and did not provide the names of these witnesses. I have contacted Mrs. Dell Stringfield on two occasions explaining that Len had intended to provide the names of the witnesses. She indicated she was remodeling her house and the files were not available. She was friendly and indicated that perhaps sometime in the future I could review them.

Note: *A two-week clean-up by the recovery team would imply that a craft or debris was found. The identity of the recovery team members is key to the case. The body was flown out on Wednesday, January 18th, and the next day, a heavy snowstorm started. Ten inches of snow closed McGuire and Fort Dix Friday, Saturday, and Sunday. When I returned on Monday, a huge mound of snow was piled up in the aircraft parking area. It was twenty feet high and about forty feet in diameter. Someone was standing on the top of the pile in a green outfit. I took a photograph, which I still have, because I suspected something was hidden underneath the snow.*

WILLIAM G. WEBER

BOMARC NUCLEAR MISSILE DESTROYED IN 1960

A nuclear-tipped Bomarc missile and Shelter 204 were destroyed in a disastrous fire on June 7, 1960, near Lakehurst Naval Base on Fort Dix property. This area is eleven miles east of McGuire Air Force Base. These three adjoining military facilities form a 21-mile-long by 6-mile-wide complex across central New Jersey. Although the Bomarc nuclear warhead burned, it did not explode. The shelter, surrounding structures, and soil were contaminated with weapons-grade plutonium. The area is now fenced off and covered with concrete. Exposure to the radiation can cause cancer to lungs, bones, and liver. Various cleanup proposals have been studied for 35 years. There is regular UFO activity in the area that seems focused on the former Bomarc Missile Site and the nuclear storage area at McGuire. Airborne gamma and neutron detectors are able to measure radiation. Numerous sightings, abduction reports, and animal mutilations in the area might be explained by radiation testing.

UFO'S – SIGHTINGS---REPORTS - COVER-UPS

1979 SIGHTING NEAR BOMARC SITE

I received a sighting report by two witnesses dating from 1979 on Route 539 near the Bomarc missile site. The witness claimed he had taken an excellent close-up 8 mm movie of a UFO as it slowly lifted off the ground. He called McGuire, and an Air Force General met them and asked for the film. The General agreed to develop the film but called later to tell them the film was damaged. The film was never returned to its owners.

FORT DIX INVESTIGATION

I have made inquiries with the Military Police, base historian, environmental engineering, the library, hospital, and base commander's office. I was able to obtain an excellent map of the area from the Army. Fort Dix is a training base open to the public. Only a few areas on the base are restricted, and several public roads pass through the base. The only newspaper reference, on January 20, 1978, two days after the shooting, was the Fort Dix announcement of the closing of roads due to a crushing snowstorm and vandalism. The Courier Post stated: "Public access along the portion of Browns Mills Cookstown Road on Fort Dix is now restricted. It is closed to traffic from 10 PM to 5 AM."

WILLIAM G. WEBER

FORT DIX UFO SIGHTING:

Twice in recent weeks, I contacted Sergeant First Class Mark Skarupa, who had an interesting sighting at Fort Dix in August of 1975. Although this sighting was several years earlier, his testimony provides inside information on police activities. Mark Skarupa now lives in Silver Spring, Maryland. He was formally in the 275th Military Police Battalion at Fort Dix, New Jersey.

Sergeant Skarupa was Shift Chief on duty on a hot summer night. The Military Police (MPs) received a call about midnight from an Army Staff Sergeant cook, who lived in the military housing area of Fort Dix. This Sergeant claimed he saw a low-flying disc in the area behind his house. Two MPs were sent to investigate and also reported seeing the object. The cook and two MPs saw a UFO at close range. They agreed its shape was like two saucers fitting together at the rim. Sergeant Skarupa jumped into his car and raced to the scene. When he reached the housing area, he also saw the object moving above the houses. It climbed in an arc like the bottom of a football. It was different from anything he had ever observed. It was moving slowly and then suddenly shot higher into the sky at a 70-degree angle at a high rate of speed. He saw it join five other very bright UFOs in the sky. He told his MPs to make out reports for each witness.

He returned to his office where he could still observe the six bright UFOs through the trees for the next four or five hours. He phoned both Lakehurst Navy Base and McGuire Air Force Base radar sites and asked if they had any radar returns. The radar personnel at both sites denied having anything unusual on their equipment. The objects held their relative position throughout the night, but were gone at sunrise. The Sergeant called the Lieutenant Duty Officer in Air Traffic Radar Control at McGuire Air Force Base. He asked, *"Did anything unusual happen last night?"* The Lieutenant responded, *"An Army helicopter went down last night at Fort Dix!" Sergeant Skarupa was startled and angry. He said, "How come you never notified the Fort Dix Military Police? No one notified us that a helicopter crashed?"* The Air Force Duty Officer then refused to respond and hung up.

Sergeant Skarupa then drove to the area behind the cook's house, but there was no evidence that anything had crashed or even landed at Fort Dix. A week later, he decided to make copies of the Police Incident Reports to keep for his personal records. He was unable to find the Incident Reports or anyone who knew what happened to them. He was leaving the service shortly and did not want to create any problems. In summary, Sergeant Skarupa knows they saw a UFO at Fort Dix in 1975, but he can't explain why the Radar Duty Officer at McGuire would lie to him about a helicopter going down.

Note: I have obtained information from radar operators that they are told to deny they saw UFOs on their radar. Also, their radar computer is programmed to delete very slow and low altitude flying objects as well as objects traveling at several thousand miles per hour. This program effectively keeps most UFOs off the radar screens. Although UFOs are often seen by radar, they are seldom reported.

DISCUSSION OF ALIEN SHOOTING WITH SERGEANT SKARUPA:

I told Sergeant Skarupa about the shooting of an alien at Fort Dix and of the body being flown to Wright Patterson Air Force Base. I asked what he knew of the incident. He said he had heard rumors about the shooting. He confirmed that the Military Police carry a .45 caliber pistol and fourteen rounds while on patrol. Sergeant Skarupa felt a .45 caliber bullet could tear the alien apart. He stated, "You have to be a good shot to hit anything, but these bullets have tremendous stopping power and would probably penetrate several inches into an alien craft." Sergeant Skarupa speculated that a craft hit with a .45 caliber bullet might be disabled and leak some type of contamination. He stated, *"There was nothing so highly restricted on the base to warrant shooting anyone. Only the area about twenty yards from the air base fence is considered sensitive. If somebody stumbled into a sensitive area, all the police had to do was stop them and ask what were they doing there? At worst, they would take an intruder in for interrogation. The MP must have been scared to death to cause him to shoot!"*

Sergeant Skurapa felt they would keep the shooting secret. Only the Night Supervisor, the Provost Marshall, and the Base Commander would be notified. The Army would scare the MP enough to prevent him from coming forward. Sergeant Skurapa did not believe that killing an alien was a felony; therefore, they would not notify Criminal Investigation (CID). It's only a felony if you shoot a human being. They probably would not even write an incident report.

I told the Sergeant about the Fort Dix roads being closed at night shortly after the incident. He felt that was a clear indication something very unusual had happened. He stated, *"Fort Dix is a quiet base with only a few drug deals and minor thefts. They don't close public roads unless they're trying to hide something!"*

MCGUIRE AIR FORCE BASE INVESTIGATION:

I have cross-referenced the names of the Air Force personnel stationed at McGuire in 1978 who may have had some connection with the incident. I am comparing names from a 1976 McGuire phone directory, local telephone directories, the Air Force Association Directory, and the nationwide Phone Disc CD. Most of the personnel have relatively common names. Often there are fifty to a hundred people with the same name nationwide. I have made numerous calls to potential witnesses and have been able to obtain some interesting information.

438th SECURITY POLICE SQUADRON

I visited the Security Police Building and learned that the mission of the 438th Security Police Squadron changed on 12 July 1978, several months after the alleged shooting. Tactical Neutralization Teams (TNT) were formed to combat possible terrorist tactics. The highly trained teams would be deployed to respond to neutralize such situations as sniper, hostage, or barricaded individuals.

2017th COMMUNICATION SQUADRON

I met with Tom Carey, a UFO Researcher twice and Eric Mintel, a paranormal investigator in Philadelphia who have agreed to help in phoning possible witnesses. Tom has made contact with several former 2017th Communications Squadron personnel from McGuire Air Force Base. One of the contacts, Jim Wiest, now President of the Delaware Valley Opera Company, was told the story about the aliens by his friend, Sergeant Tom Patterson. In 1978, Jim Wiest remembers being told about a message in communications concerning the shooting of the alien. Jim remembers Tom saying, *"They captured one!* We contacted Tom Patterson for verification, and Tom denies any knowledge of the incident. I provided Jim with my copy of the 1976 McGuire Phone Book, and he is searching to find the names of anyone he remembers. He has contacted two other communications specialists from McGuire, and both deny any knowledge of the case.

We are also attempting to substantiate another lead from a Kathy Fox of Pine Hill, NJ, who may have information about the case. She is a friend of a Palmyra police officer who sighted a UFO on November 11, 1994, over the Delaware River. She claims to have knowledge of the alien shooting in 1978, but we've been unable to reach her.

I traveled to McGuire Air Force Base on several occasions in an attempt to obtain information from the base historians, environmental engineers, and security police. I spent several days reviewing historical files, base newspaper reports, environmental data, library files, etc. Probably my best success was obtaining the names of eighteen new security police officers and fifteen photo lab personnel. Unfortunately, the names do not include their middle initial, which complicates contacting them today.

WILLIAM G. WEBER

MCGUIRE PHOTO LAB

Shortly after the incident in 1978, I was at the **photo lab.** There was an unusual excitement in the air. One airman was holding a set of 8x10 photographs in an envelope. He made it clear these photographs were highly classified and significant. He started to show me the photographs, then hesitated and said, *"I better ask my boss if you can see the photos?"* I actually held the envelope in my hand, and now wish I had looked at them. I assumed I would get permission. A burly Sergeant said, *"No one was allowed to see them unless specifically given permission by the Commander! We'll check with him, and he'll probably let you see them tomorrow."* The following day, I was told they were in the safe and no one could see them! This incident sticks out in my memory because I had never before been refused access to photographs at McGuire. I feel these photographs may have concerned the alien, and further that someone from the photo lab still has copies.

UFO CLASSES AND TELEVISION BRING LEADS

I teach classes about five times a year concerning UFOs and my students have agreed to help in obtaining information. Captain Peter Blunder, one of my students, works at the Fort Dix state prison. He called to tell me he had talked with his friend,

Colonel Barry Nunstat, the former McGuire Director of Material for the 514th Military Airlift Wing in 1978. Barry said, "He heard rumors about the shooting several years after the incident." Colonel Nunstat told me a Lieutenant Tom Smith who was with the State Police in 1978, knew something about the incident.

NEW JERSEY STATE POLICE

I called Tom Smith, who is now with the police at the NJ Turnpike Authority in New Brunswick. Tom had gotten a letter from a retired police detective in 1985, who requested information on the alien shooting incident. He said, *"At that time I checked around the New Jersey State Police Headquarters, the Army at Ft. Dix, Division Headquarters, CID, Air Force Security Police and OSI, and could not find anything about the case."* He was reasonably sure there had never been any reports. If any reports ever existed, they had been removed from the files. He wrote the detective a reply to that effect. John Bounder, another student, was able to have the State Police files checked again last month. This search was also negative.

Tom Benson, the former NJ State MUFON Director, also attempted to obtain information from the state in 1985. He is a state employee, but his request for information was denied. Tom also talked to a Sergeant Anthony Ziegler who worked at McGuire and is interested in UFOs. Sergeant Ziegler attempted to obtain the Security Police tape recordings of the night of January 17/18, 1978. He was told the tapes had been erased.

CATHY KELLY SAW UFO THE NIGHT OF THE SHOOTING

Another witness was located through my UFO classes. Cathy Kelly, who formerly lived in Brown's Mills east of the base, works for the Public Defender's Office in Mount Holly. She spotted strange lights from a possible UFO on January 18, 1978, over Fort Dix/McGuire. The next day, her neighbors told her about the alien being shot, a crash, and that an Air Force pilot was injured. She remembers hearing discussion about a Major August Roberts or Radnor. She claims she heard a radio announcement by a General stating, "The lights observed around McGuire were not UFOs, but some type of unusual weather phenomena." She felt this was untrue, and it was the only time she's heard a General make an announcement on the radio.

Almost every day she drives on the Fort Dix road that passes next to the airbase. Shortly after her sighting, she noticed unusual activity near the base. First, she saw new lights on buildings she hadn't seen before, and a new fence being built on the northeast side of the base. Most of the activity was about a mile south of Cookstown, near a bridge and a curve in the road. This was the road closed to the public at night. Then, a new sign was placed on the fence that stated: *"Unauthorized persons could be shot if they were found in this area."*

Note: I personally doubt this exact wording on the sign. I recently traveled to the area she described. This area is near the McGuire nuclear storage site, the sewer treatment plant, and there is a strange hole in the ground. The hole is about sixty feet in diameter and over five feet deep with a metal fence surrounding it. We're in contact with base environmental to determine if this hole has any significance.

1983 UFO

John W. Braswell and his spouse spotted a UFO over the McGuire storage site in 1983. They stopped the car and watched the craft for about fifteen minutes.

TWO UFOs SPOTTED IN 1990

It is interesting that two large UFOs were spotted hovering over the nuclear storage site by Mike Gundel of Cookstown on January 6, 1990. Two Saturn-shaped UFOs hovered over the area for at least twenty minutes. Calls to McGuire and the State Police were ignored. Mike even drew pictures of the craft on his window with a grease pencil. He was convinced the UFOs were there. Don Johnson and I investigated the case and visited the area in 1990. When we asked base officials, they denied any knowledge or interest in the UFOs. (The case is in MUFON files.)

1994 UFO

The latest sighting was revealed by an active-duty Lieutenant Colonel at the base. A UFO hovered over the runway and took off at a high rate of speed on July 4, 1994. Radar viewed the spectacular event. The UFOCAT listing for the State of New Jersey lists ten additional reported sightings over McGuire, five over Lakehurst and more than thirty others in the general area.

CONFLICTING TESTIMONY

I contacted Karen Robinson, whose father had told her he had been to crash recovery sites and had seen aliens first-hand. She was in high school in 1978 and remembers her father was very shaken by this knowledge. She thought he had visited a crash site in the northern part of South America. The two are not now on speaking terms. I contacted her father Paul C. Robinson, who lives in Mt. Holly. This was difficult because his phone number was unlisted so I had to find him by using tax records.

I finally located Paul at his home in Mount Holly. He was friendly but very ill with cancer. Paul was a civilian employee who worked in 21st Air Force Safety Office as a munitions' specialist. Although he was in a position to observe and be involved in this incident, he denied any knowledge of ever seeing or hearing about aliens. He freely admitted he had been to numerous aircraft crashes and taken warheads off weapons. He spoke of munitions repair operations in Greece, Germany, Austria, and South America. He also participated in defusing munitions that were involved in various aircraft accidents. He would not admit to knowing about aliens, despite his daughter's testimony to the contrary. The father and daughter have a very different recollection of the alien story. I intend to visit him again.

SIGNIFICANT CONTACTS FROM MCGUIRE

I contacted Colonel Ken Landon in Colorado, who was the Base Commander in 1978, who denied any knowledge of an alien shooting. I also called Colonel Happy Martin in Texas, the former Assistant Base Commander. He became Base Commander after Colonel Landon. Both Colonels denied having any knowledge of the alien shooting, but both switched the subject immediately to the BOMARC missile fire and the nuclear radiation cleanup. It might have been a coincidence, but it seemed like a rehearsed answer to my questions. I wonder if they were told, "If anyone asks you about aliens, tell them about the BOMARC cleanup." In their minds, there may be a connection concerning the cleanups. They were concerned about the cleanup in the late seventies and it is still being studied. Costs are expected to be in the millions to ship the plutonium to underground storage sites.

MCGUIRE SECURITY POLICE SERGEANT INTERVIEW

On May 29, I reached Tech Sergeant Huntley Wallace, who was in the Military Police at McGuire from 1966 to 1967, again from 1977 to 1981 and finally from 1985 to 1988 when he retired. Virtually everyone he knew had been shipped out of McGuire. Even those who retired have moved away. Huntley now works up in Newark in State Corrections Department as an investigator. He is trying to get transferred to the new State Penitentiary at Fort Dix. During his last three years at McGuire, he flew with all three C-141 squadrons on the Special Air Missions, where he often guarded VIPs. He had a Top-Secret clearance and provided security for the aircraft. He spent his entire career in Security Police. After some discussion, I asked if he heard about the story of the alien being shot at Ft. Dix back in 1978. He said, "I never heard that one!" He immediately started talking about the BOMARC Missile Site during his first assignment at the base. When he was reassigned to McGuire in 1971, they said the whole area was sealed off because of some type of radiation. He doesn't have any records from the time he was at McGuire. We promised to get together in the future and talk further. I contacted the Security Police Historian **_who denies having any documents as far back as 1978._**

438th MAW COMMAND POST COMMANDER NO KNOWLEDGE

I contacted Major Dale. L. Mollenkopf, the former Commander of the 438th Military Airlift Wing Command Post in 1978, who now lives in Belleville, Illinois. When I contacted Dale, he was friendly and claimed to remember me. He does not recall any story even remotely similar to an alien being shot, nor could he think of any incident that would explain the report. He believes he would have been told when he arrived in the morning at the Command Post. He was almost always told about situations involving the base Security Police.

WILLIAM G. WEBER

BLUE BOOK REPORT

July 28, 1952; McGuire AFB, New Jersey. 6 a.m. Witness: Ground Control Approach radar operator M/Sgt. W.F. Dees, and persons in the base control tower. Radar tracked a large cluster of very distinct blips. Visual observation was made of oblong objects having neither wings nor tail, which made a very fast turn and at one time were in echelon formation. Entire episode lasted 55 minutes. - Blue Book Report

BILL GILBERT CLAIMS HIS WIFE IS BEING ABDUCTED

On April 30, I talked with Bill Gilbert who works at the McGuire AFB Filling Station. I hesitate to report the following information because I have not been able to substantiate any of it. Bill comes across as a honest person, but he makes some spectacular claims. He believes that his wife and other family members are being abducted. He knows of other families who live in the Browns Mills area near the base, who make similar claims. There are also stories of mutilated deer and other animals found in the woods. Much of Bill Gilbert's information comes from Bill Van Hise, the former Mayor of Jobstown. Bill Gilbert further claims that a large underground base exists, somewhere on the three bases. Another friend of the Mayor allegedly saw a huge concrete door slide open. It was the entrance to an underground tunnel and strange circular aircraft flew out. Allegedly, some exotic liquid frozen fuels are used on McGuire and at a similar base in Scotland for this strange disc-shaped aircraft. Bill Gilbert had heard stories about the alien being shot but had no additional information.

FUELS EXPERT CLAIMS JP-8 IS NOW THE STANDARD FUEL

On May 31, 1995, I spoke to Fred Belcher who retired from McGuire in 1990, where he worked for Aerial Port Squadron for eighteen years. He claims he never even heard a whisper about the alien being killed at Fort Dix. He still works at Fort Dix in Defense Fuels for the Department of Defense. They provide fuels to the base, that come by barge to Burlington, then by pipeline to Jacksonville where it is stored, and then through a pipeline near Jobstown and into McGuire. The Air Force now uses the newer JP-8 fuel for its aircraft. There are plans to go to Commercial Jet Fuel A. The new fuel could explain part of Bill Gilbert's story of "exotic, liquid frozen fuels."

WILLIAM G. WEBER

LAKEHURST INVESTIGATION

I traveled to Lakehurst Naval Base on several occasions and met with Commander Jessie Parnell. Lakehurst has some of the largest hangars in the world. They were built to hold dirigibles such as the Hindenburg. One hangar I visited is used to store classified Army Delta Force supplies including many of its helicopters and special equipment. Commander Parnell claims he has no knowledge of a UFO base in the area. He frequently flies locally and has not seen anything suspicious. He had previously checked into UFOs and was told by his commander that all UFO related matters are handled by the National Security Council.

DISC LANDS AT LAKEHURST

Vince Creavy, the NJ MUFON State Section Director, claims that just prior to Desert Storm a disc-shaped craft landed at Lakehurst en route to the Middle East. This craft is believed to belong to the Army and is used as a reconnaissance drone in battlefield situations. This craft has a porous airfoil that acts upon the boundary air layer providing high performance with a relatively small and quiet engine. At least some of the disc-shaped craft in the area are apparently man-made.

UFO'S – SIGHTINGS---REPORTS - COVER-UPS

HARRY FROM TELEVISION IS MEMBER OF RECOVERY TEAM:

I hosted a local TV show called "Investigations UFO" in Atlantic City for 40 weeks. In March, after appearing on my television show, I was contacted by a person named Harry, who did not provide his last name. Again, this information is unsubstantiated, but it does agree with Len Stringfield's Recovery Team witness.

Harry claimed to know all about extraterrestrial craft because he was part of a Recovery Team. He alleged that the Air Force was the only organization given the job of tracking down these craft. Harry spent 19 years, from 1966 to 1986, in Site Management and Control (SMAC) at Nellis AFB. His job was to retrieve electronics from the craft. According to him, there were 27 crashes, and ten UFOs were recovered intact. Dead aliens were called DEXTERS, and live ones were called LEXTERS. He claimed to have seen 30 LEXTERS, but they died quickly. They supposedly ate overripe fruit because they needed the fructose. They could digest the fructose as crystalline sugar, which is found in sweet fruits and honey ($C_6 H_{12} O_6$). This is also called fruit sugar.

The UFOs, he said, were propelled by magnetic generation. They converted the hydrogen molecule to onboard magnetic generation. They were often seen near bodies of water because they used this for fuel. Their electrical equipment ran on extremely low voltages. He indicated he would contact me again. He did not comment on the McGuire/Fort Dix case. He claimed the craft are now in storage in New Mexico.

Note: *This location has been confirmed by other intelligence sources from Wright Patterson. The telephone operator at Nellis AFB denied the existence of any unit at the Nellis named SMAC. However, he indicated I might try bases further North such as Tonopah Air Force Base. Interestingly, Nellis AFB had a big build-up in 1966, so this lead was worth checking.*

I also visited Dr. Eric Kelson, a chemist, at Princeton University, who made a quick analysis of the fructose diet. Fructose is basically used for quick energy and occurs in fruit, honey, and is the sole sugar involved in human semen. He felt most life forms would need to supplement their diet with nitrogen found in legumes, various minerals, and some type of fat. Fat contained in blood would provide the living fat cells. If you're really interested in getting the fats and nourishment from blood, you could form a circulation system where you screen out the fat lipids and collect them. Assuming Harry is correct, abductions and mutilations may be a method to obtain blood and fructose.

UFO'S – SIGHTINGS---REPORTS - COVER-UPS

WRIGHT-PATTERSON AIR FORCE BASE:

I traveled to Wright-Patterson Air Force Base where the alien body is believed to have been taken. I met with Dr. Bill Elliott, a historian at the Air Force Material Command Headquarters, Bruce Ashcroft from the National Air Intelligence Center, and Master Sergeant David Menard at the Air Force Museum. They seemed willing to help in our quest but claimed they had no knowledge of the incident or aliens. They have searched appropriate files without success. They have provided the biography of Colonel Caudry, who is alleged to have debriefed the Security Police personnel after the incident.

I had given Dr. Elliott a tape of the May 28, 1995, Sightings TV program per his request. The show covered the possibility of government-built UFOs. He wishes to search his files for possible confirmation, particularly now that the new Avro disc aircraft (Canadian disc development) files are being downgraded.

Bruce indicated the Little Green Men are an inside intelligence joke. Nazi prisoners of war painted green men from German folklore on the inside walls of the Air Technical Intelligence building.

WILLIAM G. WEBER

DISC AT WRIGHT-PATTERSON:

Previously, I interviewed Phil Cursco, a former Wright-Patterson Office of Special Investigations (OSI) agent, who claims to have viewed a 30-foot disc-shaped UFO at Wright-Patterson Air Force Base in the early fifties. He provided the exact location and description of the building at Wright Field. It is probably the only non-hangar building on the base that could handle a UFO. He claims the government attempted to back-engineer the craft without much success. The craft and bodies were sent to New Mexico in 1979. His speculation is that the Department of Energy might be involved along with a private corporation. They took the program away from the Air Force because the government leaders felt the military would want to build up our defenses at an exorbitant cost like the Star Wars defense system.

WASHINGTON, D.C.:

I met with Richard Hall and Mike Swords, both Ufologists, and spent several days in the National Archives as well as visiting Bolling Air Force Base to check unit histories. Richard has agreed to contact the family of our key Security Police witness and arrange for another interview. The 438th Military Airlift Wing secret history does not mention the alien incident, but it does state the base was hit by a heavy snowstorm, and that there was an Operational Readiness Inspection that month. No one remembers the Readiness Inspection, which is unusual.

7602 AIR INTELLIGENCE GROUP RECOVERY TEAMS:

The primary mission of the 7602nd was to conduct worldwide human resource intelligence collection functions during the seventies. This unit is probably responsible for handling the cleanup operations at Fort Dix/McGuire for the incident. The 7602nd is believed to participate in the collection of fallen space debris that is known as Project Moon Dust. Although this unit's history is not available, I have been able to obtain previously classified documents from its third-generation predecessor, the 4602nd Air Intelligence Squadron. Unit names change whenever a unit changes to a different command. However, a unit's mission and function generally remain the same. The 4602nd records indicate this squadron was responsible for UFO investigations throughout the country. The 4602nd was composed of 61 officers and 133 enlisted men strategically placed throughout the continental US. They were located at key Air Defense Command (ADC) bases such as McGuire Air Force Base. A total of 17 flights was authorized with two officers and five airmen at each location. The primary wartime mission was to reach the crash site of downed enemy aircraft in the quickest possible way. During peacetime, they trained for war by investigating UFO cases. (These documents are available on request.)

General Ben Chidlaw, the Commander of Air Defense Command, stated in 1953: "We have stacks of reports on flying saucers. We take them seriously when you consider we have lost many men and planes trying to intercept them."

According to unit records, the 4602nd became the primary collection point and investigative body for the Air Force concerning UFOs. Project Blue Book, located at the Air Technical Intelligence Center (ATIC) Wright-Patterson AFB, Ohio, was primarily responsible for public relations. The three or four personnel at ATIC were ineffective and needed help. The 4602nd was designated by ADC to investigate and collect reports, while ATIC would analyze and evaluate the reports. This 1953 tasking authorized the 4602nd to spend both time and money on their investigation. Their mission grew to include Recovery Teams for Mogul balloons and later for space debris.

Captain J. Cybulski was assigned as the primary UFO officer within the squadron. His briefing statements during the annual Commander's conference are very enlightening.

He stated: *"The primary reason for our participation in this program is to solve a very perplexing problem for the Air Force and the country as a whole. To the Air Force, the investigation of the UFOB is very important."* Later, he mentions that *"an astronomer and the scientist were ready to quit their position at the Air Technical Intelligence Center until the 4602nd was assigned the task to help investigate. The feeling is, both at Wright-Patterson and Washington, that we could be very instrumental in bringing this thing to a successful conclusion."*

The UFO community has often speculated on the possibility of crashed saucers and stories of quick responses on the part of Military Recovery Teams. The documentation shows that this unit investigated hundreds of sightings. If a UFO did crash, this unit had the mission, manpower, and capability to reach the crash site effectively and quickly. Furthermore, the 4602d was specifically tasked to collect physical evidence such as occupants, photographs, material, and hardware. In 1959, the unit was transferred from Ent Air Force Base, Colorado, to Fort Belvoir, Virginia, and most likely kept its UFO recovery mission.

We have obtained over a hundred pages of 4602nd documentation that could probably justify a separate study. These documents prove the Air Force had a comparatively large staff working on the UFO problem and took them seriously. It is likely the Recovery Team was stationed at Fort Belvoir and could reach McGuire in about four hours driving time or in little over an hour by helicopter. We plan on contacting members of the recovery teams.

WILLIAM G. WEBER

SUMMARY OF PROGRESS REPORT:

I have initiated numerous actions that may help in our quest for the truth. I have visited Fort Dix and Fort Meade Army Bases, Lakehurst Naval Air Base, and McGuire, Bolling, and Wright-Patterson Air Force Bases to establish contacts and obtain information. I have sent 'Freedom of Information' requests to the Air Force Office of Special Investigation (OSI) and History offices and gained knowledge of the base personnel and military procedures that concern the case. There is also superficial knowledge of the incident by residents in the area. We are working to obtain additional eyewitnesses of the alien at McGuire. I interviewed a witness who claims he saw craft and bodies at Wright-Patterson in 1953. We have three other secondary witnesses who claim friends saw the bodies. I believe with perseverance we will find other key eyewitnesses. We have also uncovered several significant UFO sightings involving the three-base complex.

When I question former military personnel about the alien shooting, they often switch the conversation to the BOMARC cleanup operations. It seems like a rehearsed response. The two cleanup operations may be associated, at least in the mind of the potential witnesses.

UFO'S – SIGHTINGS---REPORTS - COVER-UPS

SUMMARY OF EVENTS:

On Wednesday morning, January 18, 1978, there were as many as a dozen UFOs in the area being picked up on radar and reported visually. A UFO became disabled over Fort Dix, and its occupant was allegedly mortally wounded by John Samuels. Somehow, the alien was able to get through the fence and died on McGuire AFB. The body was guarded by Security Police and OSI, and later a special Recovery Team arrived to handle cleanup operations. Later that day, the alien body was flown by C-41 to Wright-Patterson AFB. The next day a snowstorm started, and personnel were sent home early, and the work schedule was canceled for Friday, Saturday, and Sunday. Key roads on Fort Dix were closed due to snowdrifts, but these roads remained closed to the public from 10:00 PM to 5 AM for several months. Cleanup operations continued for several weeks, which may have involved the craft or debris. According to two separate reports, the alien body was sent to a New Mexico hospital for study in 1979. We are still attempting to verify. Our search for evidence has just begun, but I believe the case warrants a full-time investigation.

WILLIAM G. WEBER

A recap of the event...

Major Filer had gotten up early that day. He had arrived at McGuire at about 4:00 AM, where he was stopped at the gate. Normally, he had been recognized and allowed to enter. Today was different. He was stopped and asked to show his credentials, as the base was on full alert. He went in early to prepare for the daily briefing, as he was the Deputy Director, 21st Air Force Intelligence. "I was the intelligence briefer, and like every other morning, I was to put together an 8 a.m. intelligence briefing to update my bosses on the 21st Air Force operations," he stated. He drove the main road through the base toward the 21st Air Force command center. Looking out into the darkness to his right, he saw red and blue emergency lights flashing near the runway near the Fort Dix fence line.

One thing was certain: All those emergency lights were not normal. Something had gone wrong out there in the dark, and George's job was to find out and include it in his morning briefing. George accelerated and headed toward the command post.

There were reports that radar had spotted unknown targets during the days leading up to and including today. It was mentioned that around 13 targets were seen flying around normal air traffic. George had heard of the radar indication, but nothing was said, available, or written about the subject.

UFO'S – SIGHTINGS---REPORTS - COVER-UPS

During my interview with Major Filer, I asked him what he thought about the unknown craft that had been seen and reported in the past and those reported now, in the years following the 1978 event. I asked him if these craft are manmade or extraterrestrial. George stated he didn't know -- they could be both. I asked about the radar sightings during the week of the event and if anyone there took them seriously. He stated that the radar personnel did take them seriously; however, they were told not to talk about it.

I asked George about the alien. I asked how he was able to get down to the ground. Was it with a pod or something else? George stated that he thought the craft, not the pod, was disabled and landed. He also thought the alien crew could have been at least three crewmen.

Following is the report of the event that Major Filer had put together and given to me so that it would be included in this chapter. It gives details of the January 18, 1978 event.

WILLIAM G. WEBER

INCIDENT AT FT. DIX

According to John Guerra, who wrote in his book Strange Craft, The true story of an Air Force Intelligence Officer's Life with UFO's (Bayshore Publishing Co. 2018) and also direct testimony from Major George Filer during my interview with him on April 26, 2023:

"No one knows for certain from which direction the UFOs approached the Joint Base McGuire/Dix complex shortly after midnight. Did they silently approach from the south, floating at treetop level between the towns of Browns Mills and Pemberton? Or did the discs come in from the north, sliding in across the New Jersey Turnpike and North Hanover Township? Perhaps the UFOs had lined up with the runway and approached like other aircraft, running the final approach to avoid raising alarm. Or maybe they dropped straight down from the stars, halting just above the tree tops inside the secure military installation. What is known is that around 2 a.m. on Jan. 18, 1978, UFOs were flying about the base. They had seemed to focus their interest in this complex where American nuclear warheads were stored."

"Military personnel from both bases, which are separated by a security fence, witnessed the strange craft during several hours of heavy UFO activity. Fort Dix military police took up chase on foot and in vehicles, driving toward the hovering UFOs which appeared at one location and shot off and reappeared on the other side of the base complex."

"The UFO's activity was nothing when compared to what occurred in the hours following. A Fort Dix MP shot and killed an alien, entity or something. Major Filer's job was to provide details of the event to the commanding general at that morning's 8 a.m. briefing."

"He was concerned and thought had an aircraft crashed on takeoff or landing? His experience in the KB-50J aircraft in England educated him to that possibility. Or had an aircraft blown a tire and skidded to a stop after leaving the 10,000-foot runway. Weather probably wouldn't be the cause of an accident. The pre-dawn temperature was 26°F, normal for January, and there had been no snow or rain, just cloudy. The National Weather Service data for that day shows visibility of 10 miles with a light wind gusting to 20 mph NNE. He thought this was nothing to endanger flight operations."

When Major Filer entered the command post, he saw Air Force personnel at their screens, communicating with aircraft and ground personnel. "There were also a couple of Majors and Lt. Colonels in there directing air traffic," George said. "The senior master sergeant runs everything from who sweeps the floors to organizing staff schedules and making sure the phones and faxes are up and running," George said. "It is normally very dark in the Command Post early in the morning, but the lights were very bright that day."

"I was immediately met by the senior master sergeant who ran the command post that night. I noticed the senior master sergeant was agitated, excited, and his face was pale, and his eyes were open wide. 'An alien has been shot at Fort Dix and they found it on the end of our [McGuire AFB] runway,' he said. I wasn't sure what I had just heard, so I asked, 'Was it an alien from another country, like a Mexican or other foreign national?' He then replied: 'No, it was from outer space, a space alien. There are UFO's buzzing around in a pattern like they're mad.'

'A C-141 is coming in from Wright Patterson Air Force Base to pick the alien up. We need you to brief the general and staff about it at the 8 AM briefing,' he said."

"There I was, standing in the 21st AF command post, and the person in charge had just told me that an alien had been shot at Fort Dix next door, and the alien had apparently escaped and either jumped over the perimeter fence or had crawled under it to get away," George said. "And now the body had been found on the runway of McGuire AFB. And that's why all those emergency lights on vehicles were flashing out there."

"As the base intelligence officer, it was my job to gather the facts and brief the commander of the 21st Air Force. I was told that it was my job to prepare the brief. I felt I needed more information, so I called the Security Duty Officer. There was confirmation that an alien had been found by a Security Policeman. The alien had been shot on Ft. Dix, and they had alerted the New Jersey State Police and Army personnel to track down the alien."

UFO'S – SIGHTINGS---REPORTS - COVER-UPS

Alleged messages sent by McGuire AFB

UFO/Sighting/Incident Inactive Runway #5 MAFB,
N.J. 09864 Date 18 Jan 78 HOUR 0315hrs.
N.J. State Police Wrightstown Barraks, N.J.

INCIDENT/COMPLAINT REPORT

On the above date and time it was reported to this office that there were reports of UFO sighting over the base and an incident in progress on the Ft. Dix installation. Also, MAFB control tower, AIC R XXX reported same.

Upon further investigation, it was reported that an unidentified being, had been shot by Dix MP's and same entered MAFB at above location.

Further investigation revealed that there was some kind of body found on our installation.

Area was cordoned off and ECP set up. USAF clinic personnel

advised and dispatched accordingly. Recovery team notified

and responding. All necessary personnel have been notified.

See further 1569's for more information. Investigation pending.

C. EVIDENCE

One body of unknown origin released to the care of OSI
District Commander and Special Recovery Team from Wright-
Pat AFB.
Col. Lauduc
Brig. Gen, Brown
AFOSI

"Actual copies of incident complaint report in the files with the New Jersey State Police:

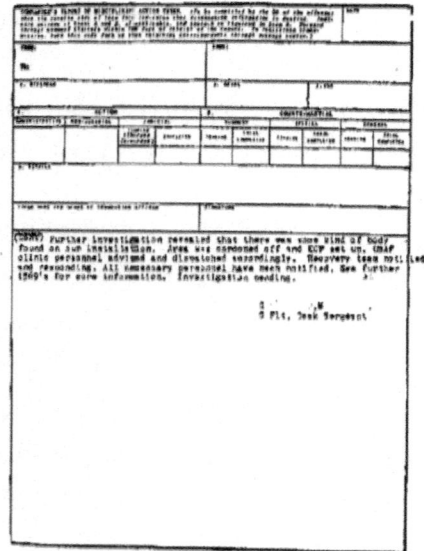

During one of his many interviews then, and now, as they still continue today with multiple agencies and news outlets from many countries, Filer later told ABC News: 'Our security police went out there and found the alien at the end of the runway dead.' During my interview with George, he could not recall any follow-up with that news agency because of the lapse of time combined with him being contacted by multiple agencies. Now, getting back to his intelligence responsibilities, *"They asked me to brief the general staff,' he said. I also called the 438th Military Airlift Command Post, who told me the UFOs were in the pattern, the tower could see them, radar was tracking them, and an alien had been found. Medical personnel were sent to try to save him."*

"In any case, something extremely strange had happened, and the base was chattering about it," George said. **"So I started calling around to the security office and the wing command post to determine what exactly had happened. And everyone had the same story -- that an alien had been shot and picked up by an Air Force cargo plane and flown off base."**

"Major Filer went on to provide more details of that night.

'When I arrived at the command post, I was told that an aircraft was coming, and that the body was still out on the runway. A special team had arrived from Washington DC to clean things up.

'I was not allowed out there, but after a C-141, supposedly from Wright-Patterson AFB in Ohio, landed and parked, an ambulance was used to drive the body out to the C-141. I talked to a flight

surgeon, who was a colonel, who knew a little bit about the scene. He told me that medical personnel had picked up the container and hand-carried it from the ambulance to the plane.'

Air Force people are highly trained, experienced personnel responsible for the safety of aircraft and people in the air and on the ground. Some of these aircraft are tasked to carry some of the biggest secrets in the military, such as the nuclear weapons for the advanced bases for Army and Air Force.

George stated: 'They aren't a group to speak openly about events.'

"Although I had heard countless Air Force pilots tell me about strange, high-performing aircraft during my career, I had seen one myself in England. I was skeptical upon hearing that an alien had allegedly been shot and killed at my job," -- "But as I interviewed base personnel, everyone told the same story."

"George was a little concerned that the air traffic controllers on base would not take his questions seriously about the current activities relative to the recent event.

'The tower people told me that the UFOs were buzzing around after midnight,' George said. 'They could see more than one UFO at a time, too. They were disc-shaped. They didn't say any of them landed.'

Tower personnel not only saw the UFOs dashing above the bases, the UFOs were also tracked on radar. Other Air Force pilots radioed the tower that they had seen the UFOs, George said.

"At the risk of repeating myself, here is the story that was gleaned from the Ft. Dix MP:

Shortly after 3 a.m., a Fort Dix military policeman saw a UFO land in a secure area not far from McGuire. Allegedly, an alien got out of a UFO or an escape pod. The MP got out of his truck and looked up. A UFO was hovering just above him. He described it as oval-shaped, with no details, and glowing with a bluish-green color. Simultaneously, a short humanoid figure stepped into the headlights of his idling vehicle. The 'thing' was about four feet tall, grayish-brown, fat head, long arms, and slender body. The MP pulled his .45 and told the intruder to stop so he could apprehend him. The humanoid continued to move and in his excited state, he shot the figure. He watched in disbelief as the thin creature ran. He also shot up at the vehicle that was hovering above him.

Years later, on June 10, 2007, The Trentonian (a New Jersey newspaper) published an article describing the ongoing belief among UFO investigators that the events at Fort Dix/McGuire AFB represent a real encounter with an alien. The reporter, Rick Murray, had gotten his information from an unnamed source familiar with the event."

OTHER STORIES EMERGE...

"We don't know why the army security policeman shot him, but at this point, the MP may have been close to panicking, especially after seeing the object over his truck," George said. *"He ordered the thing to stop and he didn't stop. One version of the story I heard is a UFO came down or an escape pod landed or crashed and the being got out. It had also reportedly occurred in a secure area, perhaps a motor pool, where vehicles were parked."*

"The security policeman hears Leonard Stringfield, a noted Ufologist, on the radio talking about UFOs a couple of years later while stationed in the Far East and he decided to contact him," George said.

The McGuire Air Force Base security policeman, who now uses the pseudonym "Jeff Morse" to protect his privacy and civilian career, wrote an account of the night's events for Leonard Stringfield, the Director of Ohio Mutual UFO Network (MUFON).

Morse mailed Stringfield a letter describing what he saw that night. Morse didn't know how the UFOs came into the base; he was amazed to see them.

WILLIAM G. WEBER

Letter Morse sent to Stringfield:

Leonard Stringfield was the director of Civilian Research, Interplanetary Flying Objects (CRIFO), and published a monthly newsletter, ORBIT. In 1957, he became public relations adviser for the civilian UFO group, National Investigations Committee On Aerial Phenomena (NICAP), under the direction of Donald Keyhoe, a friend since 1953. From 1967 to 1969, Stringfield served as an "Early Warning Coordinator" for the Condon Committee. During the 1970s, he wrote a number of books about alleged crash recoveries of alien spaceships and alien bodies.

After Stringfield learned that George had been the intelligence officer at McGuire at the time of the shooting, he arranged for George to interview Morse by phone. But that would come later.

In his letter to Stringfield, Morse provided more details on the UFOs and stated that many more people were involved in the search for the intruder alien.

According to Morse's letter, after the Fort Dix MP fired up at the UFO, "The object then fled straight up and joined with 11 others high in the sky. This we all saw but didn't know the details at the time. Anyway, the thing ran into the woods towards our fence line and they wanted to look for it. By this time several military patrols were involved." After being shot, the being then either climbed over or under the fence. When a New Jersey State Trooper radioed the McGuire AFB security office and requested entrance to McGuire's back gate – #5, to let the trooper in, this was granted. After searching with flashlights, the state trooper and Morse found the body of the alien, depending on who one asks, either kneeling in death or sprawled on its back. Either way, it was dead.

WILLIAM G. WEBER

By Richard H. Hall, Chairman of the Fund for UFO Research and editor of the MUFON Journal, the Journal of UFO History, and the book The UFO Evidence. He had asked Major Filer to write a book together.

PROLOGUE: Richard H. Hall writes, "This article originally was drafted as a sample chapter for a proposed book on the 1978 McGuire AFB case. It seemed important to report for the record what I have found out so far. Having met the primary witness on numerous occasions and corresponded with him over many years, I have a full picture of his family background and professional career. Today he has a Master's Degree in Human Relations and a B.S. in Business and Management, both from major universities. He has cooperated fully, answered all questions, and provided important details as well as leads to additional information. On one occasion when he lived in Virginia, I met with him and his wife and colleagues at their home. On another occasion, Len Stringfield (who requested my help in his investigation and introduced me to the witness) arranged for him to meet with my brother, Bill, and Dr. Bruce Maccabee. Later, the witness agreed to the taking of a formal legal deposition which was witnessed by, among others, Don Berliner and Rob Swiatek of the Fund for UFO Research. Richard Hall asked me to work with him in writing a book about the alien and he died before we could finish the book and I also spoke with the key witness. This Prologue is necessary in order to make it clear that the witness is a known quantity. At this point there is no doubt in my mind whatsoever that the report is authentic, and since it literally represents a case of corpus delicti it is of first-order importance.

The fact that several of the officers involved have denied other investigators having any knowledge of the incident is not surprising at all under the circumstances. I have long since concluded that this case is so important and held in such complete secrecy that it will take a thorough Congressional investigation to pry loose the full story lose.

Here, then, is the story of the incident that literally changed the life of a conscientious young air policeman who was carrying on a family tradition of police service, and who later was subjected to repeated threats and intimidation for talking about the experience to Len Stringfield and me.

As the night wore on into morning, Sgt. Jeff Morse and his Air Force security police partner, Sgt. Mark Larimer, were patrolling their assigned area on the grounds of McGuire AFB, New Jersey, an important Military Airlift Command base that housed combat aircraft and nuclear weapons. As members of the 418th Security Police Squadron, they were responsible for base security and law enforcement. What started out as a routine--almost boring--11:00 p.m. to 7:00 a.m. shift assignment gradually took on nightmarish qualities as time passed and began to resemble something out of the Twilight Zone. By about 1:00 a.m., they had checked the off-base housing areas and the main base, performed some building checks, and were settling in for a peaceful evening. Everything seemed in order. Morse could afford a little time to reflect on how well his chosen career was developing. Several of his family members had been in law enforcement work, so Morse was carrying on a family tradition. He had been assigned to McGuire for OJT (on-the-job-training) in police work for just over a year, since graduating from Air Force law enforcement school at Lackland AFB, Texas. He had also undergone combat training at Camp Bullis Training Center in San Antonio. The assignment at McGuire was for three years. At age 18, he considered it a privilege to be guarding such an important base. The night of January 18, 1978, was crisp and clear, the air very cold, windy, and dry. The stars were sparkling brightly. A gibbous moon hung in the sky, due to set about 8:00 a.m. The military patrol car, a sedan, had a balky heater, so Morse fiddled with it trying to get it adjusted. Although he often worked alone, on this night he had a partner from the security police side, Mark Larimer. Morse, whose assignment was general law enforcement, was showing him the ropes about that side of Air Force police work, which was similar to civilian police work but included base security work as well. The law enforcement and security police wore identical uniforms and insignias. Both were "Blue Berets,"

Air Force police with formal schooling, had SECRET clearances and were authorized to carry arms and to make arrests. Their boss, the commander of the security police squadron, was the Air Force equivalent of an Army provost marshal: "chief cop." The main responsibility of the security police was to guard airplanes and nuclear weapons against possible foreign agents or saboteurs. The radio linking the patrol car with the desk sergeant on duty in the command post was quiet, as it normally was at that time of night in midwinter. Not much was happening, so Morse decided to show Larimer the procedures involved in guarding base entry points such as the numbered gates. Sometime after 1:00 a.m., he radioed into the command post offering to relieve the gate guards for food and rest room breaks. The desk sergeant checked the logs, then dispatched Morse and Larimer to Gate #5 on the rear side of the base, the one gate in that area near the fence line adjoining Fort Dix. Gate #5 was a little-used gate in a very dark, remote area of the base, a miserable assignment for any self-respecting police officer to guard. The guy on duty no doubt would welcome a break.

Running Code

As they were in route to the gate, the radio suddenly crackled alive. Morse and Larimer heard a tense voice admonishing them that sightings of unusual lights in the sky flying in formation had started coming in from scattered locations; that they should be on the alert for anything out of the ordinary. At first, they treated the information as a joke, until they stopped the patrol car and got out to look up at the sky to see for themselves what was going on. High in the sky formations of odd-looking bluish-green lights were cavorting over the base.

At first, Morse and Larimer were shocked by the sight, wondering what they were looking at. It was an intriguing spectacle. They were single lights, not the familiar running lights of aircraft. And they were ''performing some pretty amazing aerobatics. The objects continued to fly back and forth, changing formation several times, passing over the base and then turning back for another fly-by. Morse counted 12 distinct objects in a formation headed south to north, and then apparently the same formation of 12 objects returning on a north to south pass. The high level of aerial activity at this time of night, including the formation flights, was totally unprecedented for any type of aircraft they knew about. Morse noted that the first formation was of two parallel lines of objects, with the individual objects staggered in line. Then two arrow-shaped formations were visible at different angles. The final formation was arrayed in a crescent shape, until the objects abruptly dispersed and flew off in different directions. What sort of aerial "fireworks" were these? After a while they stopped watching the repetitive flights and went back to work, but the sightings continued for a long period of time. Morse's friend, Bill Cleninger, another sergeant of equal rank, had been assigned dispatch duty as desk sergeant that night. On the radio, he sounded somewhat upset, confused, and very excited by the sightings. Part of his responsibility was to prioritize events for response and to issue follow-up assignments, while keeping superior officers informed of what was going on if something out of the ordinary occurred. Right now, he had his hands full as the UFO reports continued to pour in, confirmed by personnel in the base control tower. At approximately 0330 hours, Morse heard the sirens of civilian police vehicles running code (sirens wailing and lights flashing) on the roadway outside the perimeter of the base fence line. In the distance, he could see a New Jersey State Police car passing by on Wrightstown-Cookstown Road in hot pursuit, heading in the direction of Fort Dix Army base. Fort Dix bordered on the south-southeast fence line of McGuire AFB, and security personnel of the two bases shared a radio channel to coordinate law enforcement activities. Following the state police car was a Fort Dix military police patrol, also running "Code 3," lights and sirens. Morse thought this was rather unusual since the Fort Dix MPs ordinarily never left their areas. He speculated that they must have taken a break at the nearby 7-11 store or Ernie's pizza parlor just outside of Gate #1.

At first, he and Larimer thought the police activity outside the base could have been something routine, perhaps pursuit of a speeding car from some off-base incident. Fort Dix, as an open base, often attracted traffic violators who sought refuge there while trying to elude pursuit. But then the dispatcher informed him that the New Jersey State Police were attempting to gain entry to the air base at Gate #5, near the secluded rear runway adjoining Fort Dix.

Sgt. Cleninger instructed them to proceed to Gate #5 to assist the state trooper. As they approached the gate, they heard Cleninger communicating on another frequency with the Fort Dix Army dispatcher. Both were talking very excitedly, and trying to speak with an Army MP patrol that was in hot pursuit of something nearby and, apparently, in the process of contacting the "violators." Then there was something about a shooting.

Arriving at the gate, Morse allowed the state trooper to enter the base, asking him the nature of his mission. The officer replied that he and the Army MP patrol had been chasing an unidentified low-flying object that, whatever it was, was headed in the direction of the southeast fence line. The MP had radioed a description to his base: an oval object giving off a bluish-green glow. A sense of urgency and near panic set in when the transmission from the MP was abruptly cut off. They didn't know exactly where he was or what was going on.

Sgt. Cleninger, meanwhile, informed Morse by radio that he was now in contact with the Fort Dix dispatcher by telephone. He instructed Morse to call him on the phone at the gate so he could relay what he had just been told. Over the telephone line, Cleninger told Morse that radio contact had been regained with the Army MP, and it was learned that he had had a close encounter with the unidentified object, and apparently with one of its occupants as well.

The Army MP said that, *"The object was hovering very close to his vehicle, and that out of nowhere a 'thing' (in his words), a being of some sort, had suddenly appeared directly in front of his vehicle. It was about four feet tall, grayish-brown in color, with a proportionally large head, long arms, and a slender body."*

UFO'S – SIGHTINGS---REPORTS - COVER-UPS

Badly frightened, the MP had panicked and fired five rounds from his .45 caliber pistol into the creature, and one upwards into the object hovering above him. The object responded by accelerating straight up into the night sky, apparently abandoning the wounded creature. High overhead, the object had rejoined the other eleven blue-green objects, which were moving slowly, sort of hovering in position. In fact, Morse and his partner had seen a single object joining in with the larger group of objects at high altitude, but they had not seen where it came from.

The frantic MP said that the wounded being had fled toward the McGuire fence line, but they had lost track of it there. Following orders, Morse led the state trooper to the inactive runway near the fence line where they used their headlights and spotlights to search for anything out of the ordinary. This area was only used by the Air National Guard. Several F-4 fighter jets were parked on the flight line, and several munitions storage areas were nearby. Morse inquired of the desk sergeant, asking what exactly they were looking for. The answer startled him: "Whoever or whatever the MP shot." Since it had fled toward the McGuire fence line, it may have entered the base, he was told. So, they were looking for an injured someone or something. It was getting very late, and the State Trooper and Morse drove their separate vehicles along at a crawl, windows down, getting colder and colder, their spotlights searching through the darkness.

The state trooper was getting impatient, saying that he was too busy to be playing games and that after they made a pass searching the fence line and runway, he intended to wrap it up. Seeing nothing unusual near the fence line they next headed for the area of the taxiway leading to the active runway. By now they could see Army personnel on the other side of the fence line using spotlights to search there. There seemed to be a lot of discussion, and a group forming near a particular area of the fence line where the inactive runway made a sharp right turn in an easterly direction. Perhaps they had found the mysterious person or thing, and the thought crossed Morse's mind that after all this trouble they were going to miss out on it. All of a sudden, the two vehicles abruptly braked to a stop, as their headlights revealed a motionless figure lying prone on the cold concrete in the middle of the inactive runway, about 50 feet directly in front of them.

UFO'S – SIGHTINGS---REPORTS - COVER-UPS

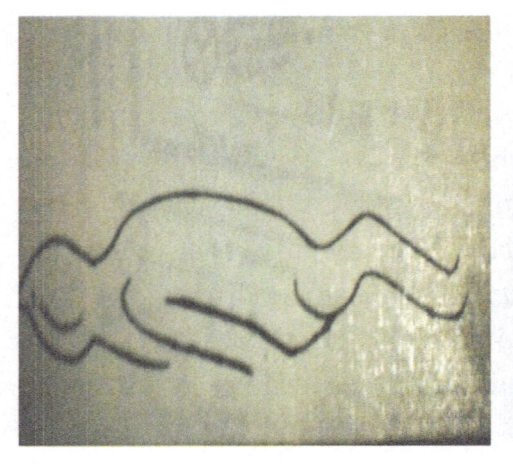

Alien sketch credit: Michael Hesemann

Represents perimeter fence where alien was found near dirt road and the runway parallel to the fence

There was no sign of how it got over or through the fence. They sat awestruck for a few seconds, then Morse grabbed his microphone and quickly informed the desk sergeant about their discovery. *"What does it look like?"* Sgt. Cleninger asked. *"It's about 4 feet in length, grayish-brown in color, with a fat head and long arms,"* Morse replied, struggling to come to grips with what he was looking at.

Morse and the trooper got out of their vehicles and were about to approach the body, noticing a pungent, ammonia-like stench in the air. As the trooper and the two security police stood side by side gaping at the body, they asked each other simultaneously, "What the hell is that thing?"

By now it was obvious to Morse that Cleninger, back at security police headquarters, was taking instructions from higher authorities and passing their orders on to him. Before they had ventured much closer to the body, he was instructed to escort the New Jersey State Policeman off the base and to set up an entry control point (ECP). The trooper protested, but this was now standard military police business: a body had been found on the base within their jurisdiction. All civilians must now leave the area. The point where it lay on the old runway was a crime scene, and it was Morse's duty to secure the area while senior officers and investigators marshaled their forces and made their way to the site. He retrieved several poles and lengths of rope from the trunk of the patrol car and began to set up a perimeter, instructing his partner, Larimer, to escort the trooper off the base.

While setting up the rope standards, Morse was joined by two additional security patrols that began to set up a perimeter to the northern side of the controlled area around the "crime scene." About this time the radio traffic became very intense, almost frantic, and they were ordered to switch to a "secure" channel. To Morse, the channel didn't sound secure. Usually, a secure channel provided a one-to-one link between the investigating officers and the desk sergeant, but in this case, it seemed to him that everyone and their grandmother were on the channel all trying to talk at once. Morse's duty was to relay information to the desk sergeant on what was happening in general, who was showing up at the ECP, and who was asking permission to enter the secure area. Authorized officials had to be separated from curiosity seekers trying to gain entry. But due to the chaotic communications, he had difficulty getting in a word at all. Individuals who were authorized to enter the controlled area were given a mathematical clearance code by the desk sergeant, assigned by protocol, and acknowledged by a simple sign language between officials and the policeman at the ECP. The code could be as simple as the security policeman holding up three fingers and awaiting a correct response of five fingers by the person requesting entry, to equal the number eight. This system allowed important personnel to gain faster access than would the cumbersome procedure of checking all IDs and asking for verification of their authorization to enter the area. For security reasons, however, the code would only remain valid for about 30 minutes maximum. It would be continuously changed or upgraded according to the level of security prevailing.

Within 30 minutes of their finding the body, Morse saw a group of about a dozen security police that he first took to be law enforcement "augmenters" arrive in a step van and take charge of the investigation, but that didn't make any sense. The new arrivals did not look or act like augmenters at all, whose normal role would be to back up the regulars. They would have arrived one by one, not in an organized group, and would have been assigned to the perimeter while the regulars conducted the investigation. Furthermore, they were armed with M-16 rifles and grenade launchers. They weren't the recognizable professional investigators of the Air Force Office of Special Investigations (OSI) either. In the Air Force police "augmenter" system, law enforcement police cross-trained on the security police side at times. On this fateful night, Mark Larimer was cross-training as an "augmenter" for regular law enforcement. Law enforcement personnel also conducted investigations, but in the event of a felony or major crime would be pre-empted by the OSI. Organization charts and procedural matters like these would take on new importance to Jeff Morse later on, while trying to understand what he observed that night.

Although the armament of the newly arrived security police might not have been unusual if the senior officers thought some kind of serious base incursion was threatened, heavy weapons were kept in an armory and would not have been readily accessible on such short notice. Morse was armed only with a .38 revolver. On the radio, he heard the special group referred to as the "recovery team." He had never encountered them before. Manning his ECP some distance away, Morse watched as senior officers and emergency personnel arrived on the scene and the recovery team went through a seemingly well-rehearsed procedure. Morse also noticed that they were all senior enlisted men, wearing the chevrons of rank but no patches or insignia that would identify their unit. He wondered what was going on but was primarily occupied in performing his assigned duty and didn't give that much thought to it at the time. In the next 24 to 48 hours the "strangeness" level increased, as a number of peculiar events transpired. Only then did Morse begin to piece together in his own mind that he must have been involved in something of a truly extraordinary nature. All he knew at the moment was that the body did not appear human.

Nearby, the McGuire runway connects to the apron in front of a former New Jersey Air National Guard hangar. On the far side of the hangar, facing the runway, is a building marked "Weapons Storage." This is not the nuclear weapons bunker; as it is no longer in use.

"Morse and the state policeman came across the body," George said. "Morse said he called in to the security command post at McGuire, telling his supervisor, 'Hey, there is a body out here.' The security commander spoke to the state police officer and told him that the matter was now in Air Force jurisdiction and that the base would handle it."

According to George, the state trooper left, leaving the Air Force security officer alone with the deceased figure on the runway. "An ammonia smell came from the area of the body," Morse told George.

Essentially, in his letter to Stringfield, Morse confirmed what George had learned:

"We found the body of the thing near the runway. It had apparently climbed the fence and died while running," Morse wrote. Morse also wrote Stringfield about the smell. "There was a bad stench coming from it too. Like ammonia smelling but it wasn't consistent in the air."

Shortly thereafter, a special team of investigators arrived dressed all in black from the Washington DC area to the site.

"It was all of a sudden hush-hush and no one was allowed near the area," Morse wrote Stringfield. *"We roped off the area and Air Force Office of Special Investigations came out and took over. That was the last I saw of it."*

"That day, a team from Wright-Patterson AFB came in a C-141 and went to the area," Morse continued. *"They crated it in a wooden box, sprayed something over it, and then put it into a metal container. They loaded it in the plane and took off. That was it, nothing more was said, no report made and we were all told not to have anything to say about it or we would be court-martialed."*

The former Air Force security officer provided more details when George interviewed him over the phone.

"He was out there alone guarding the body, when a bunch of guys in blue military fatigues and blue berets arrived in a C-141 from Wright-Patterson AFB," George said. "They said something like, 'You can leave now.' -- "They were very nasty toward Jeff. He felt he had been out there in the middle of the night; it was cold and he was guarding the body. He moved back some distance but didn't leave."

According to the Air Force, blue berets were at one point assigned to elite Air Force base security units.

Morse also told George that one of the soldiers who arrived on the C-141 used a garden sprayer to coat the alien body with a clear liquid. Several of the blue berets then wrapped the body in plastic sheeting and built a wooden crate around it. They put the wooden crate with the alien body into an aluminum box the size of a military casket. Other accounts indicate the aluminum box to be much bigger, perhaps 10 feet square.

They loaded the wooden crate (with or without the exterior aluminum container) onto an ambulance and drove it to the aircraft, which was some distance away. The plane took off, returning to Wright-Patterson AFB in Ohio.

The remains of crashed U.S. Air Force planes and retrieved foreign air and space technology are taken to Wright-Patterson Foreign Technology Division, where military accident investigators can comb over them. It is alleged that the crashed Roswell saucer and the remains of alleged aliens were also flown from New Mexico to Wright-Patterson in July 1947.

George felt it odd that a C-141 had come from Wright-Patterson; he knew no C-141s were stationed there. He called a friend at Wright-Patterson who, in fact, confirmed that a C-141 had left the Ohio base for McGuire after midnight.

Morse told George that he and other McGuire security officers were flown to Wright-Patterson two days later, where intelligence officers questioned them for several hours. They had Morse recount what he saw, describe what the alien looked like, and other details.

At the end of the debriefing, George said, Morse was told not to tell anyone of the night's events. EVER, and he and several others were immediately shipped overseas!!

"In effect, he was told if he said anything he would be killed," George said.

When Morse returned to McGuire AFB, he was told he was being transferred to Okinawa. The few people involved were transferred or retired. Those notified about the alien were in 21st Air Force and Security Police. Control Tower and radar personnel knew the UFOs were around. 99% of base and wing personnel were not notified. Those who knew about the incident were transferred or retired.

As George – who had Top Secret clearance, wrapped up his calls to tower personnel and his interviews with others in the command post, he was now prepared to brief Major General Tom Sadler on the events of the morning. Just before I gave my briefing, I was told not to brief about the alien that the Commander of the 438th Security Police Squadron. Lt. Col. Frank Mazurkiewisz would brief him, alone in his office, George said.

At this time, he didn't have much information so soon after the event, just that the command post sergeant and tower personnel had told him that UFOs had been flying around both bases, that John Samuel, a Fort Dix MP had fired his weapon at a strange intruder, and that the intruder had made his way onto McGuire AFB, where it died. People on the base were calling the intruder an alien being.

The entity had been flown to Wright-Patterson on a C-141, and was now off-base.

UFO'S – SIGHTINGS---REPORTS - COVER-UPS

George put together what he had and walked to Sadler's office. As he neared the office door, he stopped in front of a wall mirror to adjust his tie and uniform. Sadler insisted anyone entering his office use the mirror to check his appearance before entering. I could see the 418th Security Police Squadron, Lt. Col. Frank Mazurkiewisz talking to General Sadler. He was wearing camouflage clothes and needed a shave.

"Shortly he walked up to me and said, 'George, we don't need you to brief the general on this. I've already briefed him.'"

General Sadler waved me in and I handed him a Top-Secret Code Word Notebook with interesting intelligence that he read in about ten minutes. This information should not be briefed out loud and can only be read due to its high classification. It was a silent brief, a 'Read Only' report," that I provided General Sadler most mornings. The general quietly reads the material – that way extremely sensitive information can't be picked up by listening devices." We exchanged a few words but nothing about the alien. George said. The daily 8:00 a.m. verbal briefing in the Command Post can only be classified Secret level or below. This briefing is similar to your national evening news with numerous slides, maps and an occasional video telling of the possible threat to our aircraft or personnel. Air Force 1, the President's aircraft and support aircraft are under 21st Air Force Command. I often prepared flight plans and clearance for the top White House personnel including the President.

After the morning briefing, George often went to the McGuire AFB photo lab to get the latest images taken by military personnel to use in the briefings. I went in the back of the photo lab and an airman who I was friendly with had an envelope with the latest photographs taken during the night stating, "You won't believe these."

He handed me the large 8 by 10 envelope and I started to open the envelope. "Just has George started to pull out the pictures, a junior officer said, "He is not cleared for those photos." Suddenly he reached out and grabbed the photos. "He can't see these," George remembers him saying. George, who had Top Secret clearance, told the officer he planned to brief General Sadler and needed the photographs. The officer stood his ground. And said, I'll check with the Commander to see if you can see them. This was the only time in several years I was refused permission to see their photos. It is likely the photos were of the creature, which apparently had been photographed as it lay on the unused runway.

Years later, after General Sadler retired, George called him at his home in the Carolinas. George asked him how he was doing, reminisced a bit, then asked, He said, he might be coming to New Jersey to visit a car racing track. As New Jersey Air Force Association state president, he asked General Sadler 21st Air Force Commander if he would come and speak to our members perhaps about the alien situation, "If you want to talk about the alien, you'll have to come North Carolina to my home do it," George quotes Sadler as saying. "I don't want to talk about it over the phone."

UFO'S – SIGHTINGS---REPORTS - COVER-UPS

Following are excerpts from **Leonard Stringfield's 1985 MUFON Symposium Proceedings, *June 28th, 29th, and 30th, given at St. Louis, Missouri.***

"In March of 1981, Leonard Stringfield was preparing for one of the papers he was writing. He felt that he would need to have an assessment of the cases he was working from outside friends, as he was receiving controversy of the pros and cons of his UFO crash recovery and retrieval work. He invited two of his closest friends: Dr. Peter Rank – Chief of Radiology at Methodist Hospital, Madison, WI, and Richard Hall, former Assistant Director of NICAP and Editor of the MUFON UFO journal. After some discussion over a weekend, it was decided that the McGuire AFB incident was most important. It was necessary to confirm the credibility of witness Morse. Richard Hall was given Morse's information so he can communicate with him. On April 10, 1982, Hall sent a certified letter to Morse. Communication seemed to be one-sided, where after some time, Morse would respond.

Approximately 17 months later, On September 27, 1983, Hall received an urgent letter from Morse. In that letter, Morse went on to say that he had been warned, threatened, and interrogated in February of 1983, because he chatted with Stringfield. On October 10, 1983, and again on November 30th, Hall had written again. Morse contacted Hall by phone on December 6, 1983. Morse stated that two days after the event, he was summoned to Wright Patterson AFB, Dayton, Ohio, for interrogation. Soon after, he was transferred overseas to Okinawa. Others involved were sent overseas as well. Morse indicated that he would respond to Hall's questions by letter. On December 14, 1983, sketches of the body and a rough area map were included. During the phone calls with Hall, Morse provided names and ranks of the officers who interrogated him at Wright Patterson. Toward the end of December, Hall received an incident/complaint report signed by a Desk Sgt. and a 1st Lt. which was forwarded to Col. Landon – Commanding Officer of McGuire AFB and also Brig. General Brown, 21st Air Force at McGuire, as well as the Air Force Office of Special Investigations (AFOSI). It contained the names of the security policemen involved, which included Morse and the name of the MP, who was identified by Morse as the individual who had shot the alien.

For the incident itself, which occurred at McGuire AFB, we only have Morse's word that it happened the way he described it, based on his observations and real-time experience. Upon completion of his military service, Morse contacted the New Jersey State Police for their involvement in the incident. He got nowhere. He stated that they wouldn't cooperate. He couldn't locate the Trooper who was involved as well.

"As I mentioned earlier, there were several stories out there from "credible" newspapers, etc., that went on to say this was a hoax.

Following is a sampling of them: This one was printed in "The Skeptics UFO Newsletter," by Phillip J. Klass– SUN #73, Fall 2002, Copyright 2002

UFO'S – SIGHTINGS---REPORTS - COVER-UPS

NIDS (National Institute for Discovery Science) Concludes That McGuire AFB "Dead-ET" Tale Is A Hoax Which Challenges Earlier Claims By MUFON's George Filer The claim that an Extraterrestrial (ET) was shot to death on the night of Jan. 17-18, 1978, at the McGuire Air Force Base (or adjacent Army Fort Dix) is a HOAX, according to an investigation by the National Institute for Discovery Science (NIDS). The NIDS finding which challenges the claims of George A. Filer, who reportedly was a USAF intelligence officer at McGuire AFB at the time - [SUN #68/Summer 2001]. Filer, who is MUFON's Eastern Regional Director and produces a weekly Internet web-site on UFO reports, was one of the star witnesses at Dr. Stephen Greer's first major press conferences for his Project Disclosure, held May 9, 2000, at the National Press Club. Results of the NIDS investigation were posted on its web-site in mid-July, but have been ignored by Filer's own web-site (as of late August).

The dead-ET tale was first made public by (the late) Leonard Stringfield in his paper presented at the 1985 MUFON conference. He was first informed of the incident via a letter received on Sept. 23, 1980, from a James Morse (pseudonym), who said he had been a military security officer at McGuire at the time, when he claimed that there had been numerous UFO sightings in the area. Roughly two months later, Morse wrote again to say he now had retired from the USAF and the two men then corresponded intermittently. Three years later, Morse called Stringfield on the telephone and in a subsequent phone conversation Morse claimed that he and others involved in the incident had been flown to Wright-Patterson Air Force Base two days after the incident. They were interrogated about the incident. Morse had even provided the names and ranks of the (alleged) interrogators. Shortly afterward, Morse said, that he and the others involved were transferred from McGuire to distant overseas air bases. Soon after this disclosure; Morse sent Stringfield – a photocopy of official Form 1569 –." Incident/Complaint Report," which seemingly confirmed Morse's story about the dead-ET who (allegedly) had been shot by a military policeman whose name was listed. Stringfield's 1985 MUFON paper, which is available on the NIDS web-site, indicates he had ambivalent feelings about the veracity of Morse's story. But when Richard Hall, a long-time UFO researcher and former deputy director of NICAP had the opportunity to interview Morse in person on Jan. 13, 1985, Hall reported finding him credible, this prompted Stringfield to make public the dead-ET story at the 1985 MUFON conference.

ALLEGED DISCLAIMERS

In response to several requests, NIDS deputy director Dr. Colm Kelleher, whose specialty is "cattle mutilations," tasked special investigator Roger Pinson to investigate the case. During the following few weeks, Pinson talked to dozens of persons by phone and communicated with many others via email, as summarized on the NIDS website. Because the incident reportedly had occurred 22 years earlier, some records had been discarded, but Pinson was able to locate and interview several former key McGuire AFB officials.

Results Of NIDS Investigation: *(Skeptics UFO Newsletter – Fall 2002)*

UFO'S – SIGHTINGS---REPORTS - COVER-UPS

The NIDS investigation found NO corroboration for the reality of the dead-ET incident. It discovered evidence that the Form 1569 Incident/Complaint Report that Morse provided was so flawed that it probably was counterfeit. NIDS' Pinson interviewed the former Lt. Colonel whom Morse claimed had interrogated him at Wright-Patterson Air Force Base about the incident. The officer, who had been based at McGuire AFB at the time, flatly denied that he had ever been to WPAFB.

"One initial expected outcome of this report may be a number of voices claiming NIDS is naive and 'of course senior military people are going to deny all knowledge," NIDS admits. But it adds, "Four senior military officers who were stationed at McGuire AFB at the time of the incident were interviewed by NIDS investigator Roger Pinson who had extensive training in interviewing and interrogation techniques as well as the detection of deception .... The four military officers responded without hesitation and further, they insisted that they should have known about the incident if it had occurred. (SUN Comment: If an ET had been shot to death at McGuire AFB, this base and Fort Dix would have been mobilized for a to-be-expected ET reprisal attack. But this did not occur.)"

NIDS investigated the reported shooting of a non-human entity - *Fort Dix/McGuire AFB, 18 January 1978 - the NIDS investigation – by NIDS Investigator Roger Pinson. Pinson was asked to do a review of the case on July 18, 2000*

Shown below are the report notes of Roger Pinson:

1) Found that Stringfield had been advised on January 1, 1985, that all DD forms 1569 for the location and period involved had been destroyed.
2) Located and interviewed the "former commander of a McGuire AFB squadron." In fact, he was the only squadron commander on the base. This individual had been at the base on January 18, 1978. He denied any knowledge of the incident.
3) Spoke to a "former" McGuire AFB, AFOSI Commander, at the base in the 1980/81 time frame. This person had never heard of the incident.
4) Located and interviewed another former McGuire AFB AFOSI commander. This man was at McGuire in 1978. He said he never heard of anything remotely resembling a UFO sighting or shooting incident involving an alien while he was at McGuire.
5) Heard from a Captain Denise Waggoner of the 108th Air National Guard, who advised that she had interviewed a Sergeant Morse of the 438th Security Forces, "who told her that he remembered no such incident occurring in 1978."
6) Found that the name of the Fort Dix MP who allegedly shot the alien was given as "John Samuels." Pinson located phone numbers for 67 John Samuels in the

USA. He called all 67, contacted 42, but none were the individual sought.

7) Spoke to former Colonel Landon, former base commander of McGuire in 1978, whose name was mentioned on the DD1569. Landon stated that there was no such incident.

Pinson's report concluded:

"The four main people on the base in 1978 who should have known of a UFO sighting were interviewed. None of them claim to know anything about the alleged sighting or alien close encounter."

In summary, the following appeared on the NIDS website:

NIDS consulted a retired senior member of the 438th Security Police Squadron about the DD1569 form. "Seven separate discrepancies were found on the DD form 1569 by the senior security police officer. These discrepancies led to his opinion that the DD form 1569 in question did not describe a real incident and was probably a forgery."

Morse claimed that he was interrogated at Wright Patterson AFB by an individual. Morse gave his rank and name. NIDS located this man and interviewed him. This man advised he was associated with JAG at McGuire AFB at the time. "...but (a) he had never heard of the incident, (b) he had never been to WPAFB at any time in his life, and (c) he had no knowledge of any interrogation of Morse."

NIDS confirmed that a Jeffrey Morse had worked as an E4 at McGuire AFB, but was unsuccessful in locating him.

"NIDS working hypothesis...is that the 1978 McGuire AFB incident did not happen."

Author's Note: Is this the typical scenario of a government cover-up, trying to keep the public in the dark about events that were and still are happening worldwide, or are there groups that tend to discredit folks who have seen and reported what they have seen??

In ending, Dr. Bruce Cornet who worked for NIDS feels it is an organization paid by the government to cover up any real serious UFO events. The Base Commander is in charge of buildings, cleaning, feeding, and housing, not in operational command so he may not have been told or is simply lying if he knew. Apparently, NIDS found several discrepancies in DD form 1569 filled out by Jeff Morse to explain the incident. The witness - George Filer (Major USAF, retired), who was stationed at McGuire AFB in 1978, serving as the Deputy Director, 21st Air Force Intelligence, is prepared to testify on what he knew then and moving forward, what he has learned since about the incident.

NIDS never contacted me, Major Filer. Unless I was a known friend of ranking persons, no one revealed info about aliens to

UFO'S – SIGHTINGS---REPORTS - COVER-UPS

me. Jeff Morse was interviewed by five NICAP personnel and they felt he was truthful. NIDS claims they contacted the only squadron Commander on base.; There were multiple Squadron Commanders on base including three C-141 Airlift Squadron Commanders none of whom were briefed. Jeff Morse was interviewed at Wright Patterson AFB by several men in street clothes who may have had a similar name to the McGuire JAG. General Sadler, who knew me, would only talk about the aliens at his home in North Carolina. Multiple Air Police denied knowing anything or would not reveal what they knew. Anyone who had knowledge was threatened from death to losing their pension, etc. Fort Dix: 780 MP Battalion, E-4 John J. Samuels, 275th, MP. - Gunman?

In August 1975, E-7 Mark Skarupa: Silver Springs, MD. 301-585-5163 who was in the 275th Military Police Battalion at Fort Dix, He was shift chief on duty during the 2300 to 0700 hours shift. The MPs received a call from an Army Mess Staff Sergeant about 2330 hours in the western military housing area of Ft. Dix. This Sergeant claimed he saw a low flying disc in the area behind his house. Two MPs went to investigate and also reported seeing the object. Sgt. Skarupa went to investigate and when he reached the housing area was shown the object. It climbed higher in the sky and appeared to move in a slow arc like the bottom of a football. It was moving slowly and suddenly shot higher into the sky at a 60-degree angle at a high rate of speed. He then could see six very bright stars in the sky. These were much brighter than surrounding stars and in an unusual pattern. Later that night, he saw the same six bright stars still hovering in the same relative position despite the fact that the normal star pattern had moved across the sky. The three earlier witnesses claim to have seen what appeared as two saucers fit together at the time. The Provost Marshal, two saucers together, asked if they had anything on radar. He called both Lakehurst and McGuire radars to inquire about radar returns. Both radars denied having anything unusual on the radar. Toward morning he called the Lieutenant duty officer in Air Traffic control at McGuire Air Force Base and asked if he had anything unusual happen last night? He responded that an Army helicopter went down last night at Fort Dix. The Sergeant said, "How come you never notified Fort Dix MPs? No one notified us that a helicopter had gone down." The Air force Duty Officer then refused to respond. It was now daylight so Sergeant Karupa then visited the area behind the Mess Sergeant's house but there was no evidence anything had landed or crashed. Ask Mark did they carry 45's, Who was there later?

I've contacted both the Ft. Dix and McGuire Historians who have no knowledge of the incident. Note most historical files are at Air Force Historical Research Agency, Maxwell AFB Archives, 205-953-5342 Capt. Mills and Petter. Contact 7602 AIR INTELLIGENCE GROUP Ft Belvoir, VA for requesting Photo **Imagery.**

CIVILIANS:

On April 30, I talked with Bill Gilbert who works at the McGuire AFB gas station. Bill claims that McGuire AFB has special exotic fuels for strange aircraft. These fuels may be for the F-117 and B-2 Stealth or Aurora aircraft. However, these particular aircraft were not operational when I heard similar stories in the late '70s. Much of Webster's information comes from Bill Van Hise 265-8170 former Mayor of Jobstown refused to talk to me. Bill Webster claims that a large underground base exists somewhere on the Fort Dix/Lakehurst complex. There are several rumors about this effect. Trenton Banks supposedly loaned money to builders to start this underground project. Joe Stefula has heard that special liquid frozen fuels are available in Scotland possibly for the Aurora. Allegedly, some type of special fuel line runs in the back of this man's house Dix, NJ. This sighting occurred along the route between the two bases.

Peter Blunder one of my students in my Southampton Schools class called on November 2, 1994, to tell me he had talked with his friend. Colonel Barry Nunstat. Barry had been the Director of Material (DCM) of the 514th Military Airlift Wing at the time of the incident. He had not heard about the death of the alien at the time of the incident. However, he did hear rumors about the story several years later. He thought Lt. Tom Smith, who was with the State Police at that time knew something about the incident. Tom is at the Turnpike Authority in New Brunswick. (908) 247 0900. (Ext. 5517) I called Tom on March 1, 1995. He had gotten a letter from Faucet a retired police detective, 1712 Main Street Coventry, CT 06238 in 1985 who requested information. He checked around the State Police Headquarters at Ft. Dix, Division, CID, OSI, AF Security Police and could not find anything about it. I visited the State Police Headquarters at Fort Dix, who claimed no knowledge of it.

WILLIAM G. WEBER

Additional information from Major Filer's memories...

I started looking for more evidence of the UFOs in the snowstorm that occurred and found a huge pile of snow about ten feet tall with a security policeman guarding it that could have hidden a UFO or an escape pod or part of a UFO. The snow pile was fairly close to the runways where the alien was found.

During the incident, a State Policeman was searching for the alien in his police car with Airman Jim McCaughan in his Air Force vehicle when the alien body was found, and he was asked to leave McGuire immediately. The Air Police Command Post indicated an Air Force Security Policeman, Jim McCaughan was out on the runway guarding the alien and that a special recovery team had arrived to take over. They either were flown to the area or were aware of the UFOs much earlier in the evening.

Years later with the help of researcher Leonard Stringfield, I interviewed Airmen McCaughan who had found and guarded the body. During the last several years prior to Len Stringfield's death, I talked to him numerous times about the case. Shortly before his death, Len told me McGuire may be potentially the most important case because of the government's continued denial of the Roswell, New Mexico UFO crash. Len claimed he had talked with Major's daughter whose father was the pilot of the C-141 that carried the body back to Wright Patterson. The Major knew there was an alien body on board his C-141 Test Squadron aircraft from Wright Patterson but had not seen it. I particularly wanted to talk to him since I had flown the C-141s, several thousand hours.

UFO'S – SIGHTINGS---REPORTS - COVER-UPS

After being debriefed at Wright Paterson AFB, within days the Airman was transferred to Okinawa. McCaughan was very frightened and stated, "That this would likely be the last time you'll see me." He wishes to be identified as Sgt. Morse.

Len Stringfield felt the alien could have been involved in a crash of his craft or had just ejected from a pod or cockpit of the UFO. Unfortunately, Len passed away and did not provide the names of the pilot witnesses. I have contacted Mrs. Dell Stringfield on two occasions explaining that Len had intended to provide the names of the witnesses to me. She never found them. I have been the NJ State MUFON Director for over twenty years. I have contacted several generals and hundreds of people concerning the McGuire/Ft. Dix incident about the forgotten death of the alien.

Within the last few months, after over forty years, we have connected with two new witnesses. The first is a former CIA pilot who landed his C-130 aircraft at McGuire during the night. His crew was not allowed to deplane due to a shooting incident. His aircraft was connected to a power cart to stay warm in the freezing weather. He watched all night facing the UFO area. He turned on the aircraft radios and listened to the base radio transmissions. He could see UFOs, vehicles, lights, and alien figures from a distance, as personnel in the tower also could. He and his copilot figured out what was going on as they watched and listened throughout the night.

Glen Green, MUFON's NJ Director of Field Investigators, noticed a report in the MUFON DMZ and contacted former

Corporal Carlos Cruz, who is the second witness. Carlos was riding in a jeep with Sgt. Carlos Smith on January 18, 1978, on the border of McGuire AFB, just off Texas Avenue in Fort Dix. Glen Green and I interviewed Carlos several times on the phone. He stated he was abducted early in the evening and had been experiencing missing time for several hours. He would not provide any details about the actual abduction since he was unconscious or unable to remember what happened aboard the UFO. Glen Green and I had numerous phone calls with Carlos, who thought he had been abducted on January 18, 1978, on the border of Fort Dix and McGuire Air Force Base.

Corporal Carlos Cruz was a US Army Fort Dix soldier and medic whose duties required visiting the firing ranges and treating any injuries to soldiers that may occur there. His supervisor of the ambulance jeep that evening was Sergeant Carlos Smith, a native Panamanian American.

After the incident, roads were closed at night and most people closely involved were transferred or retired. Major Filer also talked to the daughter of a soldier on the recovery team who came from the Washington D.C. area. She stated, "Her father woke her up and said we are going to McGuire tonight and they drove near the base and were put in a motel for two weeks. Her father told her and her mother that his team was cleaning up the mess implying a UFO or part of one might have crashed. The civilian road that cut through Ft. Dix was closed every night for several weeks.

UFO'S – SIGHTINGS - - - REPORTS - COVER-UPS

During my career, I frequently briefed four-star generals on UFO operations. I also flew aircraft for 5,000 hours. The autobiography of my life in John Guerra's book "Strange Craft" gives numerous details of my life. I have been Eastern MUFON Director since 2000 of 21 states and was New Jersey State MUFON Director for 26 years. I interviewed Lance Corporal John Weygandt; a Maine who examined a UFO shot down by our forces in 1999. For two years, I had a TV Atlantic City program called "Investigations UFOs".

Information obtained in Corporal Carlos Cruz' phone calls with Carlos and Glen Green:

Glen Green, NJ Director of Investigations, and I had numerous phone calls with Carlos who thought he had been abducted on January 18, 1978, on the border of Fort Dix and McGuire Air Force Base, just off of Texas Avenue and Range Road in Fort Dix. This area is near the intersection of two McGuire runways. Carlos was an Army soldier and medic whose duties required him to visit the firing ranges and treat any injuries that may occur there. His supervisor in their ambulance jeep that evening was Sergeant Carlos Smith, a native Panamanian American. They were medics covering the Ranges. If anyone got hurt, they came to the aid station or drove to the injured person. The medics worked throughout Fort Dix firing ranges. Sergeant Carlos Smith was superstitious about anything supernatural and told Carlos to go directly to Freedom Ridge. That night they were going on Range Road to Freedom Ridge when they heard a couple of shots, so Carlos got out of the ambulance to see if someone was injured. Then he saw the UFO flying around, some Army vehicles, and a civilian police car driving past.

They got on the road about 7:50 P.M. and were driving down Range road. Carlos saw lights of three possible UFOs skipping like stones over water. Sergeant Smith wouldn't look at the UFOs since he was afraid of anything supernatural. The UFO started coming down towards them. Smith said, "Keep moving and head for Freedom Ridge; if I don't see it, it's not there." Carlos, looking through the fence, could see lots of commotion. There were trees and the planes turned as they taxied to take off. They headed toward Range Road at 8:00 PM. Carlos saw a green with silver metallic UFO stop floating. Then Carlos felt something strange in his head and felt this was when they were abducted off Range Road.

UFO'S – SIGHTINGS---REPORTS - COVER-UPS

McGuire/ Fort Dix Fence, With Carlos

Several hours later, after the abduction ended, Carlos wakes up next to Fort Dix side of the fence, and Sgt. Smith is sitting next to him in the jeep still knocked out. Both medics have bloody noses. He is standing next to an 8- to 10-foot-high chain-link fence. Almost immediately, Carlos heard a shot but wasn't sure where it came from. Looking through the fence, Carlos sees two UFOs on the ground near the runways at McGuire. Carlos saw an entity crossing the fence, maybe through some opening. There were several aliens running around their craft. The closest one looked like he was terrified. They looked naked or had form-fitting clothes. The aliens were apparently looking for the missing alien. Carlos said they didn't look like they were trying to hurt him. There is another UFO hovering above. Sgt. Smith and Carlos' nose continue to bleed.

There could have been at least 3 Alien Species that were working together with various skills and technologies. At one point in the event, Carlos believed he saw 5 ETs running that reached the Air Force runway. Might the aliens' ability to go through the fence without leaving any marks represent an exotic ET technology?

Carlos saw a craft off to the left with aliens apparently looking for the alien who was shot. One is running to the craft, and they appear to be looking for their friend. Carlos saw two gray aliens in front of him, and three or four more were near the craft. He had to stay alert. Over to the right, there are aliens 4 ½ feet tall that looked kind of dirty. Most of the light was from McGuire. Carlos called "Sgt. Smith" to check him out, but he was still out. On the other side of the fence is a reddish-gray alien. Carlos looked but was not scared. He said, "It was looking like a movie, and the aliens seemed to be in greater trouble."

A craft was close to the ground but not on the ground. Carlos saw 5 or 6 grayish aliens move near him. A reddish alien was near a craft in the distance. He thought he heard more shots probably from a 45-caliber pistol. The alien on the left is gone, and the alien in front of Carlos doesn't seem right. He turned and looked at Sgt. Smith, who was looking straight ahead but not moving. I don't see any holes in the fence. Carlos sees an Air Force and civilian police car passing by. Searching appears to be going on the McGuire side. Carlos was 19 years old at the time with an alien 8 feet away, and it looked really robotic. Another alien looked natural but had no belly button. The gray, red one was smaller than the one in front of him.

Robot- was behind the fence who appeared afraid he would be shot.

He could see an alien running to the left, and something greenish behind him. Carlos felt they were searching for something, and he also felt an alien was injured. He saw the beings had large eyes, narrow shoulders, and they raised their arms, and he heard a humming sound. They were a foot smaller than Carlos with a square head, with large egg-shaped eyes. He thinks he saw a hole in its nose for breathing. More aliens came out of the craft. Carlos was now face to face with an alien. Then in his mind, he felt the anxiety of the entity and what was happening mentally to him. He felt it was running from someone and trying to return to his craft. The alien was impressed by the urgency of his search and didn't want to get shot and just wanted to return to its craft. While this was going on, Carlos looked at Sgt. Smith, who remained just sitting there in a blank forward stare. Carlos turned back to the entity to keep both within sight. It seemed like the entity wanted to enlighten him to the urgency of its survival. Telepathy Carlos thinks it was communicating with him. He could see almost everything that was going on through the alien's thoughts. There was a tremendous commotion going on in McGuire AFB, with Air Force police vehicles and a state trooper car driving erratically up and down the airfield. Carlos felt pain in his head. Someone might be shooting, or the aliens could grab him so there was danger.

Sgt. Smith suddenly awakened, so Carlos jumped into the Jeep and drove out to Freedom Ridge to be relieved by his follow-on shift. I reached the gate at the end of Range Road and the other medics. Sgt. Sal Lebrun was mad and asked, "Where the hell have you guys been!?" They got there at 12 something at night. Carlos still thought it was 7:30 PM because their watches had stopped. It was now actually 1 AM. The soldiers waiting to be relieved were angry since they had been waiting since 7 PM. Carlos and Smith claimed they lost time somewhere, which only made the other medics very angry and weren't accepting excuses.

Sgt. Smith (Smitty) has loose tissue, a bloody nose, and a severe headache, and Carlos puts him on a cot. Carlos' shift started at 2 o'clock and was scheduled to be over at 7 PM. They had four or five hours of missing time. In a couple of weeks, Smitty was transferred to Panama, and Carlos was transferred to Germany. I didn't tell anyone else. Carlos claims he did report what happened the next morning, even though Sgt. Smith kept insisting not to report it. He was still very frightened. As a matter of fact, that night when they finally got to Freedom Ridge, besides being late, he had a severe headache all night until he finally passed out. Carlos tuned the vehicle in the motor pool and was still bleeding so he went to the hospital with a cut head and pain was bad.

Carlos claims he can't get rid of the headaches or nose problems. Afterward, he had nightmares and saw a huge triangle later. He often stayed up all night worrying. He kept it secret for over 40 years except for his wife and children. He could see a craft circling around and thought this was an invasion, but he never felt scared. His life came to a head at that moment, and he heard the story on the radio, and felt it was true. Several of his kids have also had sightings later in North Carolina. Most of his kids are now in the medical field. A couple of weeks later after the incident, he was in the Pacific with bad headaches.

Carlos claims he is the rest of the story, which has never been told until now, that became the Fort Dix/McGuire AFB Flap/Incident. It's been a mystery since they never asked about Carlos' side of the story.

By George Filer, Thanks to Glen Green and Corporal Carlos Cruz

WILLIAM G. WEBER

Lukens Steel - Coatesville, PA – 1992 Incident

Coatesville, a small city in Chester County, Pennsylvania, United States, had a population of 13,350 according to the 2020 census. Located approximately 39 miles west of Philadelphia, Coatesville developed along the Philadelphia and Lancaster Turnpike in the late 18th century. It spans U.S. Route 30, known as the "Main Line" highway running west of Philadelphia.

During the early 20th century, Coatesville experienced growth with the establishment of the Lukens Steel Company and other industries. However, its population declined after industrial restructuring led to job reductions. In 1997, Lukens was acquired by the Bethlehem Steel Corporation.

Lukens Steel Company held the distinction of being the oldest iron mill in continuous operation within the United States. By 1995, it ranked among the top three producers of plate steel and was the largest domestic manufacturer of alloy-plate. It consistently ranked fourth out of 24 public steel corporations in profitability, boasting 14.8% equity five years in a row. The company specialized in producing carbon, alloy, and clad steel plates, supplying steel beams for the construction of the World Trade Center in New York and for two Nimitz-class nuclear aircraft carriers, the largest warships in the world.

UFO'S – SIGHTINGS---REPORTS - COVER-UPS

In 2002, International Steel Group acquired Lukens Steel Company, which subsequently changed ownership three more times before becoming Cleveland-Cliffs. Presently, Cleveland-Cliffs stands as the largest flat-rolled steel company in North America, continuing to produce heavy, thick steel plates.

On Wednesday, June 10, 1992, a pleasant summer day with fair to mostly cloudy skies and a temperature hovering around 80°, several employees at the steel plant witnessed an object landing in the steel yard on a steel plate as quitting time approached at approximately 4:30 PM.

Manufactured steel plates of various thicknesses

"It touched down briefly and then took off towards the old Coatesville Hospital," one worker reported, dismissing it as a mere balloon.

However, this incident sparked discussions across the company the following day.

Evelyn Walker, a spokesperson for Lukens Steel, contradicted the balloon theory, describing the object as a silver flying saucer with rotating multi-colored lights. She mentioned that a Lukens security guard also observed the unusual object above the property. Walker stated that Lukens was still investigating the incident, acknowledging the varying accounts from different witnesses.

Author's Note: *This doesn't sound like a balloon to me....*

Walker went on to say the story varies from one person to another. As a result, Lukens had not yet come up with a reasonable explanation for the report. " It takes a while to determine what it might have been, who saw it, what was being seen and how did it end ". She also declined to say whether Lukens employees were discussing the sighting, both inside and outside the company.

Lukens Steel, who is a defense contractor did not allow any UFO investigators talk with any of the witnesses or answer any further questions about what they had seen. Attempts to set up interviews outside of the plant were unsuccessful. The guard and the witnesses were intimidated and told keep silent. They were told that if they talked, they would lose their jobs. They were also told not to meet with any UFO investigators. It was alleged that Men in Black had visited with several of the witnesses and threatened them. The sighting was officially

UFO'S – SIGHTINGS---REPORTS - COVER-UPS

explained away as the **"ramblings of a drunken security guard."**

Fortunately, a statement from a Lukens employee shed light on the incident: "The UFO flew very low and slow over the guard at the gate, about 25 feet above her." The guard, described as an older, no-nonsense woman, experienced a burn-like sensation resembling sunburn after the event. She requested a transfer to a different gate due to fear, eventually leaving Lukens a few months later due to ridicule from coworkers.

A spokesperson for the Coatesville police revealed on Friday, June 12th, that no reports had been filed regarding the incident.

Author's Note: *Is silence golden?*

Over several months, attempts were made to locate individuals employed by Lukens Steel at the time of the sighting. Despite having names of several potential witnesses, none were willing to come forward for discussion, even after over 30 years. Consequently, the incident remains classified as unknown.

UFO'S – SIGHTINGS---REPORTS - COVER-UPS

Pine Bush, NY - 1997

Pine Bush is a small village located in the town of Crawford and adjacent to Shawangunk, New York, within Orange and adjacent to Ulster counties, with a population of 1,538 according to the 2000 census. It is located roughly 82 miles north of New York City.

The community was one of the four early nineteenth-century settlements in the town. It has previously been known as "Shawangunk," "Crawford," and "Bloomfield." Currently, there is another community called "Crawford," located to the northwest in bordering Ulster County. It was an early train stop for a short-line railroad, the Middletown & Crawford Railroad. This line was bought by the Erie railroad, which served the town until the 1970s. Some nearby cities include Kerhonkson, Plattekill, Middletown, Accord, and Goshen.

From 1981 to 1987, there were over 25,000 reports of a boomerang-shaped unidentified flying object in and near Pine Bush in Orange County, New York. There were so many reported sightings that this quiet hamlet became known as the "UFO Capital of the East Coast."

Alleged Boomerang traveling above Taconic Pkwy, in the vicinity of Millwood, NY in 1983. Photo taken from Unsolved Mysteries TV Video

On the 3rd of October 1997, a group of ten investigators from four states had elected to meet at Newburgh, NY for a three-day field trip. These investigators were very interested in the subject of Ufology and wanted to come together to do an experiment. Typically, field investigators do their work driven by their own preconceived notions about the subject matter at hand. The group consisted of Paranormal Investigator and UFO Researcher Rick Atristain, Dr. Bruce Cornet, George Filer, and others.

The experiment was to see if ten people could work together as one and collect data at night using various types of instruments and cameras. They also wanted to try to duplicate some of the results that were uncovered by UFO/UAP investigator Dr. Bruce Cornet, who had been studying the Pine Bush phenomenon since June of 1992.

The field crew consisted of ten individual experienced Field Investigators, who elected to meet and stay at the Super 8 Motel located in Newburgh, NY. An organizational meeting was set up at a nearby Holiday Inn.

Investigator Rick Atristain organized the project while Dr. Bruce Cornet provided the field locations for their nighttime experiment. The first location where the team set up equipment was along Muddy Kill Lane, located on the eastern side of a low ridge along the western side off the Wallkill River Valley.

Two theodolites (surveying instruments with rotating telescopes) were used to track objects in the sky, determine their trajectories, and triangulate their distances and altitudes. Communications between pilots and the tower at Stewart Airport were also recorded.

Rich Atristain provides training to the team on how to use the surveying equipment.

The Muddy Kill Lane location could not be maintained because local residents complained about the research activities. Montgomery police asked us to locate somewhere else. The police chief and Sergeant Edward Clancy offered their property, but it was not close to where Dr. Cornet had done his research. As a result, the Owen dairy farm was chosen instead.

On the Owen farm was a Native American mound, which was considered to be the UFO hotspot. Shown below is an aerial shot taken in May 1994. It shows the raised mound with a remnant hexagonal shape with another permanent circular feature to the west. It is from the small field just west of the circular feature that a UAP rose up two years earlier. Circular discolorations in the grasses can still be seen from the air, years after they were made by craft landing and taking off from there.

Probable ancient Indian Mound left, landing field right

The field between the mound and circle was measured, the theodolites set up, and the distance between them measured, and cameras on tripods positioned in order to record aerial objects from different angles. The Indian mound material consisted mostly of stream pebbles and orange-brown soil, implying that it was built up and not the product of natural erosion.

On 28 October 1995, another group of people witnessed a UAP of Dr. Richard F. Haines (Dr. Haines was a NASA research scientist, author, and Ufologist) turn on its plasma headlights, lift off from a small field to the northwest of the Indian mound, and fly to a field to the southeast of the mound.

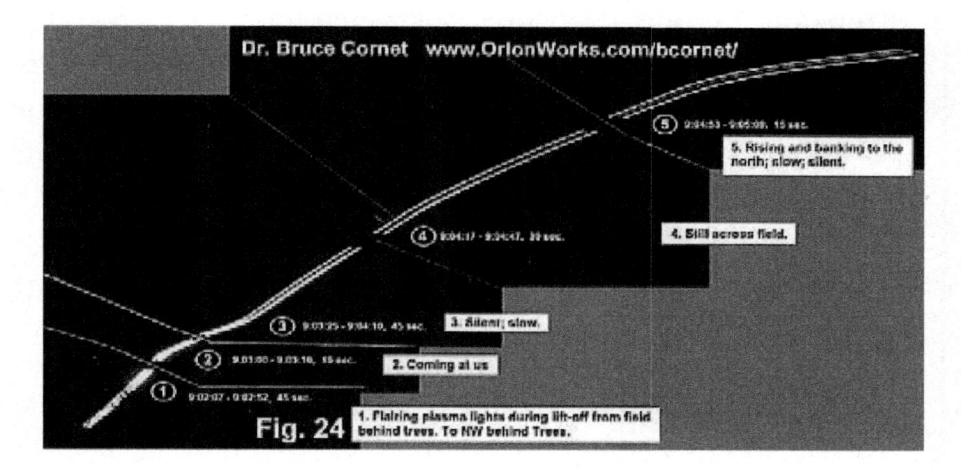

Flashing plasma lights during lift off from field, turning silent

Getting back to work performed by the team, for most of the evening, the team saw and recorded conventional aircraft either flying towards or from Stewart International Airport or flying at high altitude over the valley. If it hadn't been for the recording of a pilot asking the control tower to *"Check those runway lights up nice and bright for us,"* indicating it was not landing at Stewart, then thanking the tower for complying, implicates a human pilot and a possible military aircraft landing at a secret base nearby. No aircraft landed at Stewart at this time. Note, it has been alleged that some aliens speak English and needed runway lights.

It wasn't until Dr. Cornet had his film developed that he discovered the first two anomalies: Lights that appeared to strobe on the time exposures but which did not strobe on the video, and glowing bars of light across the leading edges of both wings. In addition, the running lights on the video appear normal: White, green, and red. But all the lights on the time exposures are a golden color. There were five still frames, showing the boomerang shape from directly below at 10:53:12 pm eventually showing it turning and moving away from the camera.

Eighteen seconds of video are presented, with the last image at 10:53:30 pm viewing the boomerang from behind. The time exposure on the right represents about 20 seconds of time, with the central strobe firing once every three seconds.

Bill Ristau, a flight instructor and airline pilot for 31 years, analyzed the pictures of this wild-looking "craft" appearing to be the "Boomerang."

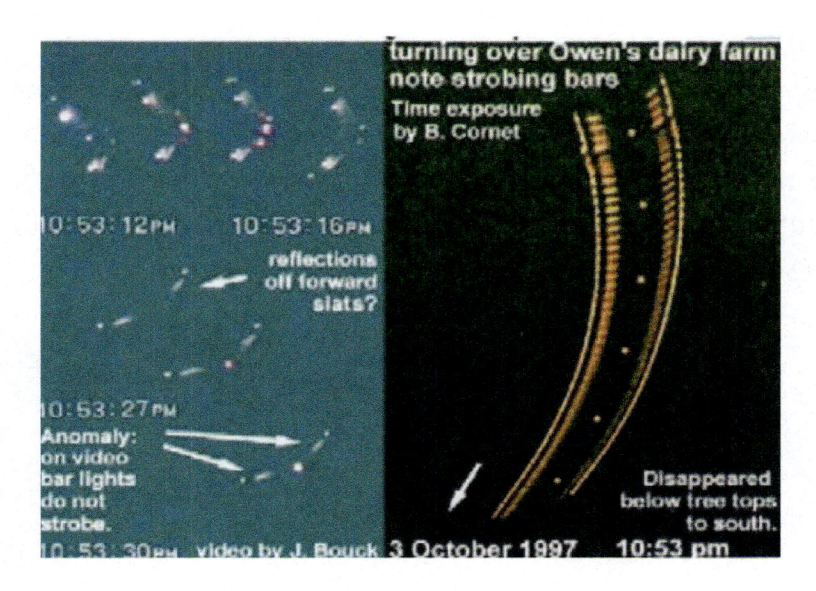

Bill Ristau, a flight instructor and airline pilot for 31 years. analyzed the pictures of this wild looking "craft" appearing to be the "Boomerang"

"The wing dihedral portends an angle of 15 to 20 degrees or more. I do not remember ever flying any aircraft with more than about 5 to 7 degrees of dihedral. Dihedral enhances stability during turns and indicates this craft has low-speed capabilities. This is speculation but the extreme angle of descent, not ending in a crash, might well be proof of that. I suppose it is not one of ours since all airports are locked down now since 9/11.

There is no reflection of light off of a forward-projecting fuselage, engine pods, and no reflection of light off of a tail section. If this aircraft had a tail and nose section, its bright lights would reflect off of some part of those structures. There is no elongate dark silhouette where a fuselage would be on a conventional aircraft.

UFO'S — SIGHTINGS---REPORTS - COVER-UPS

Instead, the fuselage appears to be trapezoid in shape, with a square, box-like front. The running lights and strobes are asymmetrically positioned, which is highly unusual – especially for so many of them being asymmetrical. The landing lights and strobes are also located too close to the center line of the aircraft; these conditions are not typical of conventional aircraft."

YouTube image at Pine Bush, NY

> If a tail and nose existed for this aircraft, its bright lights did not reflect off of them.
>
> There is no reflection off of engine pods on the wings.
>
> OCT. 3 1997   10:53:04 PM

Bruce Cornet caught this on video flying sideways over his neighbor's property in Red Bank, NJ, on 24 April 1997

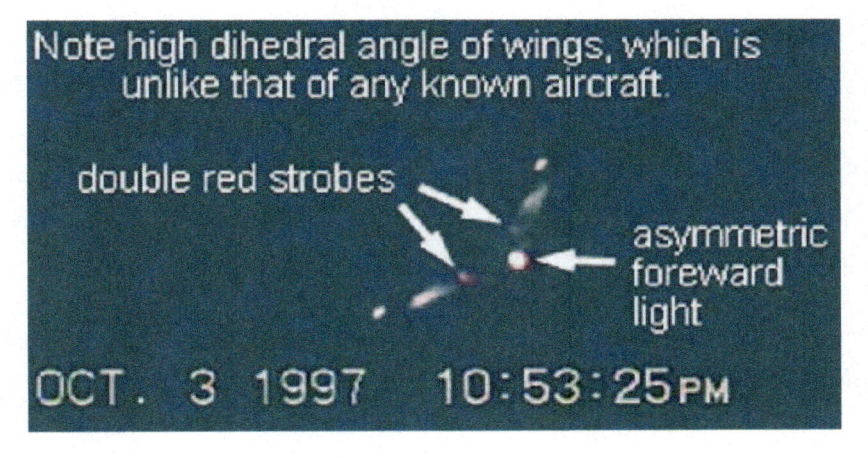

> Note high dihedral angle of wings, which is unlike that of any known aircraft.
>
> double red strobes
>
> asymmetric foreward light
>
> OCT. 3 1997   10:53:25 PM

The dihedral angle of the wings is incorrect for a conventional aircraft. As Bill Ristau pointed out above, the dihedral angle of this aircraft is 15-20 degrees or more. NO conventional or military aircraft has its wings forming a V-shape like this. The time exposure shows all the lights to be of a similar golden color. Only the central bright light, which occasionally flashes red on the video, has an aura of red around it in the time exposure. The bar-like slats along the leading edge of the wings glow and pulse in time with the wingtip lights. Forward slats on conventional aircraft do not reflect light from nearby strobes. Why are the colors so different between the two media? Why do the two bright round lights in the center of each wing not show up very well on the time exposure, along with the other colored lights? Dr. Cornet presents evidence that these types of anomalous craft can project different images to cameras positioned next to one another.

The sound produced by the boomerang-shaped aircraft resembles that of a conventional jetliner to the unaided ear. However, frequency spectral analysis reveals the very same types of characteristics noted for other anomalous craft caught on video and/or audio over the Pine Bush hotspot by Dr. Cornet between 1992 and 1997. The sound spectra are quite different from that of conventional aircraft jet engines in that there is little or no white noise as in typical jet engines.

Material for the Pine Bush story above provided by Maj. George Filer III, USAF (Retired)

The Pine Bush Boomerang has been reported by hundreds of people living in Orange and Ulster counties over the years. Ellen Crystal was one of the first people to report this type of craft in her book, Silent Invasion, (St. Martin's Press, 1996).

WILLIAM G. WEBER

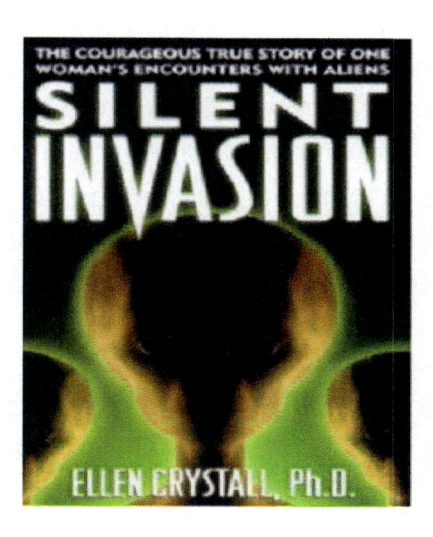

Silent Invasion is a startling, well-researched, and well-documented account of Ellen Crystall's close encounters in Pine Bush, New York. She presents fascinating explanations for many UFO mysteries and compelling photos of aliens and their spacecraft.

The recording of a pilot asking the control tower to turn up the runway lights, and then thanking the tower implicates a human pilot and a possible military aircraft at a secret base nearby. It would be possible that this boomerang flew over us when another aircraft was on approach to Stewart. These aircraft may contain long-range radar to pick up drug-carrying or enemy aircraft.

She notes that boomerangs come in small and large varieties (p. 115 – Silent Invasion). The small one is described as being about 25 feet from tip to tip, while the large one is about 200 feet in perimeter. What we witnessed at the Owen dairy farm on 3 October 1997 matches her description of the larger craft.

The asymmetrical distribution of strobes and lights (for example, the large white central light is positioned slightly off to the starboard side of dead center, and the two red strobes are not in line with one another), as well as the blue-green color of the "green" starboard light, are characteristics of these anomalous craft. - Ellen Crystal -Silent Invasion, (St. Martin's Press, 1996)

The absence of white noise and the composite nature of the frequency spectrum for its engine sound indicate that the sound recorded is synthetic and not mechanical. Similar synthetic sounds have been recorded for other Pine Bush UAP.

The recording of a pilot asking the control tower to turn up the runway lights, and then thanking the tower for complying, strongly implicates a human pilot and a possible military aircraft landing at Stewart Air Force Base or a secret base nearby. It would be possible that this boomerang flew over us when another aircraft was on approach to Stewart. The request could be a legitimate request for runway lights for the boomerang base. Bruce Tilden was stationed at Stewart Airport, photographing, and recording all the aircraft that landed and took off during the time the team made observations at the Owen dairy farm. He did not see any aircraft landing at the time the boomerang landed.

She personally talked to C-5 pilots at Stewart who had never seen a Boomerang craft anywhere. It would not be out of consideration that this boomerang intentionally flew over us when an aircraft was on approach to Stewart. The broadcast of a request to the control tower would be coincidental, giving the boomerang a great cover. Such timing has been a common ploy used in the past.

Note: Other airports such as Wallkill, located roughly 12 miles north of Stewart are also in the area with restricted entry to the public that may be used by the boomerang craft. There are no known experimental military craft with these attributes. Then it is possible these are alien craft using various techniques to disguise their operations. Two investigators spotting the boomerangs at night have red apparent burns on their faces. Sunburn is caused by UV radiation, either from the Sun or from artificial sources. (Thanks to Dr. Bruce Cornet)

UFO'S – SIGHTINGS---REPORTS - COVER-UPS

Sighting at Bethlehem, PA - 2013

A Possible Mid-air Collision

Bethlehem, PA, lies in the geographic center of the Lehigh Valley, a metropolitan region covering 731 square miles with a population of 861,899 people as of the 2020 census. It is Pennsylvania's third-most populous metropolitan area and the 68th-most populated metropolitan area in the U.S. Smaller than Allentown but larger than Easton, Bethlehem is the Lehigh Valley's second-most populous city. It borders Allentown to its west and is 48 miles north of Philadelphia and 72 miles west of New York City.

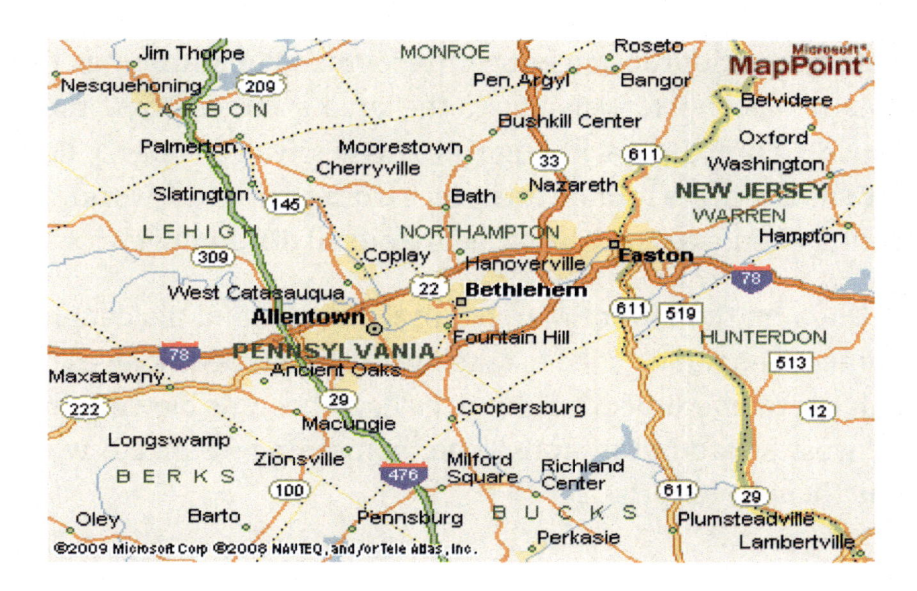

Bethlehem became a center of heavy industry and trade during the industrial revolution. Bethlehem Steel (1857–2003) was founded and based in Bethlehem. It was once the second-largest steel producer in the United States, after Pittsburgh-based U.S. Steel. SteelStacks, a ten-acre campus dedicated to arts, culture, family events, community celebrations, education, and fun, now occupies the site that was once home to Bethlehem Steel. Located in the backdrop of the blast furnaces of the former steel plant, it has been reborn through music and art, offering more than 1,000 concerts and eight different festivals annually.

The city of Bethlehem is a popular tourist destination, especially during the Christmas season. Named Bethlehem on Christmas Eve in 1741, it is rooted in holiday charm. Since 1937, the city has appropriately been recognized as Christmas City USA. It also hosts Musikfest, the area's largest free music festival, annually each August. The festival spans 10 days, attracts roughly a million attendees from all over the world, and features hundreds of musical acts from all different genres.

Then on the 13th of March, 2013, a father and his daughter (name withheld) decided to take a walk, as the weather was nice with the temperature at around 38°F, with winds blowing from the west at around 9 mph. Then, something occurred, which took them by surprise...

Actual witness testimony:

"On March 13, 2013, my daughter and I completed our walk and then went to my car, which was parked in the parking lot of the Exxon Gas Station on 13th and Broad Street in Bethlehem, PA. At approximately 8:50 PM, my daughter was saying her goodbyes when over my shoulder she shouted, 'Dad, what is that?' I turned around and, in a panic, I saw at least 100 or so round objects moving left to right slowly without a sound. They were bluish in color, and in the front, most were gathered in a formation, while others were scattered behind, some actually floating at the time. Then, as they proceeded further away, the ones that were floating accelerated almost from 0-80MPH in about 1 second or so. It was truly amazing."

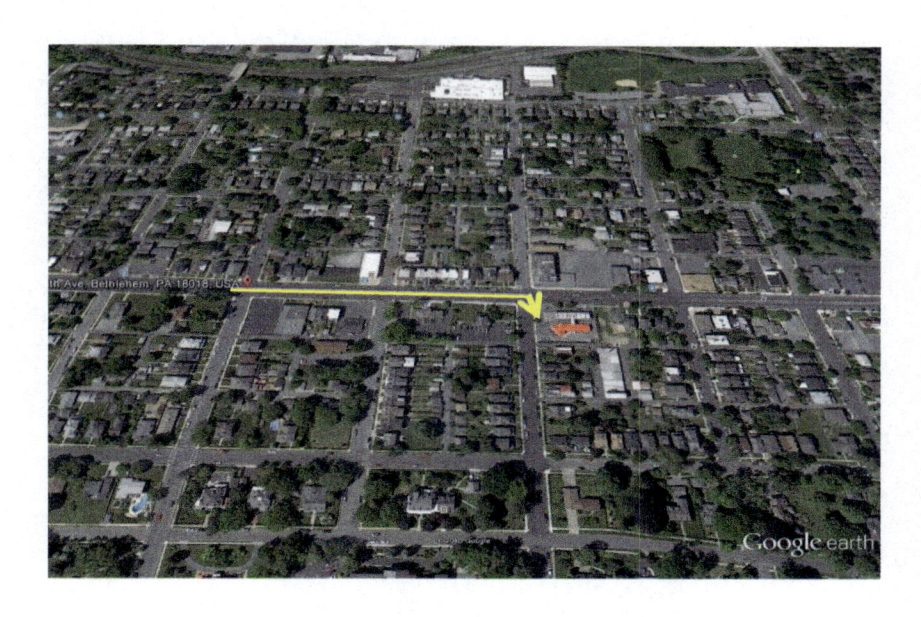

Figure 1 Arrow indicates path taken for walk

UFO'S – SIGHTINGS---REPORTS - COVER-UPS

Location of Gas Station – 13th & Broad

Location of Gas Station – 13th & Broad

WILLIAM G. WEBER

The witness reported the sighting event to us on March 23, 2013, via telephone. Based on the witness's verbal report, it was thought to be a grouping of Chinese Lanterns. At this point, there was no investigation initiated, as the witness had no way of entering his report into our database, because he did not have access to a computer. This situation was brought to my attention as the MUFON Pennsylvania Chief Investigator for the State. It was agreed that given the information collected at the scene and witness testimony, there still existed the possibility that the objects could have been Chinese lanterns. However, after some discussion and consideration, it was agreed that the incident did have merit, and the information would be entered by me. This was done on March 26, 2013, where the sighting report became an incident to be investigated. I then assigned the case to State Section Director – Dan M. on March 26, 2013, to initiate the investigation. On March 27th, Dan contacted the witness to set up a physical meeting at the sighting location. This was done on site to determine the approximate size and distance from the witness at the sighting event, which occurred over the South Mountain area.

On March 29th, Dan M. met with the witness at the sighting location and took a written statement. Weather conditions were verified for the sighting date. Dan then contacted the Bethlehem, Allentown, and Hellertown Police Departments to inquire about any reports of strange anomalies in the sky. No record of any report was given. On April 5, 2013, documents related to this sighting were sent to a second witness – Ms. Patricia D. for completion. Once completed, they were to be sent back to Dan M. As part of a standard established practice when dealing with airborne phenomena, FOIA requests were sent to the FAA and the USAF on April 10th by Dan.

WILLIAM G. WEBER

Freedom of Information Act Request to FAA

DATE REQUESTED: April 10, 2013

REQUEST SUBMITTED BY: E-MAIL   U.S. MAIL   FAX   IN-PERSON

NAME OF REQUESTOR: Dan M

STREET ADDRESS   :

CITY/STATE/COUNTY :

RECORDS REQUESTED:
"Please provide any and all records of objects in the sky both known and unknown for a period of 1/2 hour both before and after the noted time of event stated below in a 25 mile radius of Bethlehem, Pa.
Date of Event: March 13, 2013
Time of Event: Approximately 8:50PM, EST
City: Bethlehem
State: Pa.
Earth Coordinates: 40 deg 37' 19.77"N- 75deg 23' 55.22" W(specific)

Event:
Object : Multiple objects that were moving from W to E(90 degrees). The altitude was between, approximately 3-4,000ft. appeared steady at first and then began to ascend. It was last seen in the E quadrant of the sky. The objects were described as moving at a low rate of speed. The objects appeared to move West to East and then ascend rapidly.
The objects were observed for approxmately 10 Minutes
The objects made no discernable sound.
The objects were observed in the southern quadrant of the sky, almost directly overhead by several witnesses.
If you wish additional information on this please contact me.

Representatives of scientific or educational organizations - The requester represents a school or educational institution operating a program of scholarly research, or a noncommercial scientific organization operating solely for the purpose of conducting scientific research and not intended to promote a particular product or industry. The requester pays for the cost of duplication after the first 100 pages.

Fee: Negotiable

FOIA Request sent to FAA

UFO'S – SIGHTINGS---REPORTS - COVER-UPS

Freedom of Information Act Request to USAF

DATE REQUESTED: April 10, 2013
REQUEST SUBMITTED BY: E-MAIL   U.S. MAIL   FAX   IN-PERSON

NAME OF REQUESTOR :Dan M

STREET ADDRESS :

CITY/STATE/COUNTY :

RECORDS REQUESTED:
"Please provide any and all records of objects in the sky both known and unknown for a period of 1/2 hour both before and after the noted time of event stated below in a 25 mile radius of Bethlehem, Pa.
Date of Event: March 13,2013
Time of Event: Approximately 8:50PM,EST
City: Bethlehem
State: Pa.
Earth Coordinates: 40 deg 37' 19.77"N- 75deg 23' 55.22" W(specific)

Event:
Object : Multiple objects that were moving from W to E(90 degrees). The altitude was between, approximately 3-4,000ft. appeared steady at first and then began to ascend. It was last seen in the E quadrant of the sky. The objects were described as moving at a low rate of speed. The objects appeared to move West to East and then ascend rapidly. The objects were observed for approxmately10 Minutes
The objects made no discernable sound.
The objects were observed in the southern quadrant of the sky, almost directly overhead by several witnesses.
If you wish additional information on this please contact me.

Representatives of scientific or educational organizations - The requester represents a school or educational institution operating a program of scholarly research, or a noncommercial scientific organization operating solely for the purpose of conducting scientific research and not intended to promote a particular product or industry. The requester pays for the cost of duplication after the first 100 pages.

Fee: Negotiable

FOIA Request sent to USAF

On or about April 17th, Dan had received a confirmation letter from the FAA (shown above) indicating that they had indeed received his FOIA request. The FAA had then advised that he contact one of two of their offices: College Park, GA and or Renton, WA. This is typical of them; that is, to delay the information request. Finally, on or about April 22, Dan received a FOIA confirmation letter from North American Aerospace Defense Command. This letter indicated that he may receive a response back from them on or about May 20th. The letter also advised that there may be a fee attached to the request for document searches (another bump in the road). Shown below is that letter:

NORTH AMERICAN AEROSPACE DEFENSE COMMAND
AND
UNITED STATES NORTHERN COMMAND

22 April 2013

Dear Mr. Dan M

We would like to inform you that our Freedom of Information Act (FOIA) Requester Service Center received your FOIA request dated 10 April 2013. The following information about your FOIA request is being provided to you for tracking purposes:

Date Received: 22 April 2013

Requested Documents: Any and all records of objects in the sky both known and unknown for a period of 1/2 hour both before and after the noted time of event stated below in a 25 mile radius of Bethlehem, PA. Date of event: March 13, 2013. Time of event: Approximately 8:50PM EST. Earth Coordinates: 40 deg 37' 19.77"N - 75 deg 23' 55.22" W (specific). Multiple objects that were moving from W to E (90 degrees). The altitude was between approximately 3-4,000 ft appeared steady at first and then began to ascend. It was last seen in the E quadrant of the sky. The objects were described as moving at a low rate of speed. The objects appeared to move West to East and then ascent rapidly. The objects made no discernable sound. The objects were observed in the southern quadrant of the sky, almost directly overhead by several witnesses.

Assigned FOIA Case No: FY13-22APR2013-NNC42

*Fee Category: O

Expected Response Date: 20 May 2013

If you should have any questions about your FOIA request or to check the status of your request please send an e-mail to nc.foia.omb@northcom.mil and include our assigned FOIA case number.

* Fee Categories:
Commercial Use (C): Requesters should indicate a willingness to pay all search, review, and duplications costs when the records are requested for commercial use.
Educational / News Media (EM): Requesters should indicate a willingness to pay duplication charges in excess of 100 pages if more than 100 pages of records are desired.
All Others (O): Requesters who do not fit into any of the previous two categories should indicate a willingness to pay assessable search and duplication costs if more than 2 hours of search effort or 100 pages of records are required.

Kristina J Roth

KRISTINA L. ROTH
Chief, FOIA Requester Service Center

On or about May 4th, Dan received a second communication from the USAF. This communication stated:

UFO'S – SIGHTINGS---REPORTS - COVER-UPS

NORTH AMERICAN AEROSPACE DEFENSE COMMAND
AND
UNITED STATES NORTHERN COMMAND

HQ USNORTHCOM/CS
250 Vandenberg Street, Suite B016
Peterson Air Force Base CO 80914-3801

APR 25

Mr. Dan M

Dear Mr. M

We received your Freedom of Information Act (FOIA) request dated 10 April 2013. Your request was assigned USNORTHCOM FOIA case number FY13-22APR2013-NNC42. In your request letter you asked for the following: Any and all records of objects in the sky both known and unknown for a period of 1/2 hour both before and after 8:50PM EST on March 13, 2013 in a 25 mile radius of Bethlehem, PA. Earth Coordinates: 40 deg 37' 19.77"N - 75 deg 23' 55.22" W (specific). Multiple objects that were moving from W to E (90 degrees). The altitude was between approximately 3-4,000 ft appeared steady at first and then began to ascend. It was last seen in the E quadrant of the sky. The objects were described as moving at a low rate of speed. The objects appeared to move West to East and then ascent rapidly. The objects made no discernable sound. The objects were observed in the southern quadrant of the sky, almost directly overhead by several witnesses.

Our agency does not perform a mission that would result in any responsive documents relevant to your request. USNORTHCOM partners to conduct homeland defense, civil support and security cooperation to defend and secure the United States and its interests. A search of our systems of records was not conducted.

As a requester in the "All Others" fee category you receive the first two hours and first 100 pages of record at no cost; therefore, there are no assessable fees for processing your request. If you have any further questions concerning your request, please do not hesitate to contact our FOIA Request Service Center at the above address.

If you are not satisfied with our Commands' response on your request, you may administratively appeal to Mr. James Hogan, Chief, Policy, Appeals and Litigation

WILLIAM G. WEBER

NORTH AMERICAN AEROSPACE DEFENSE COMMAND
AND
UNITED STATES NORTHERN COMMAND

Branch, Office of Freedom of Information, 1155 Defense Pentagon, Washington DC 20301-1155. Your appeal should be postmarked within 60 days of the date of this letter, cite our case number FY13-22APR2013-NNC42, and it should be clearly marked "Freedom of Information Act Appeal" on the request.

CHARLES D. LUCKEY
Major General, USA
Chief of Staff

"Essentially, we felt that we were getting blown off, and I guess that the USAF didn't want us to know what they had found as a result of Dan's inquiry. Another thing to note was that their response came around one day after they acknowledged receipt of our FOIA request for information. This, in and of itself, is very unusual. See their response below:"

Our agency does not perform a mission that would result in any responsive documents relevant to your request. USNORTHCOM partners to conduct homeland defense, civil support and security cooperation to defend and secure the United States and its interests. A search of our systems of records was not conducted.

Meanwhile, back on April 26th, the second witness Patricia D. had contacted Dan and advised that she had sent completed documents to him. These documents were never received.

On May 6th, a call was placed to the second witness, inquiring about the status of the documents she stated she completed. A voice message was left for her to contact us, which she never did. Dan had contacted Daryl Nerl, Associate Editor of a local online newspaper called the Bethlehem Patch, asking him if there were any reports that the general public called into his newspaper regarding this event. He indicated there were none but had agreed to run a story soliciting any input on the 14th of May We waited, but nothing was called in. On or about May 23rd, Dan had received a CD containing radar data from the FAA. This then was sent to Glen S. (radar analyst) to decipher for us. While working with Dan on this case, in early July, it was felt the next step on our end would be to contact the tower at Allentown to see if we can obtain additional information regarding the radar data we received from Glen S. toward the end of June. If more data / testimony is available, then the case would be updated to include that data.

WILLIAM G. WEBER

Shown below is the radar data analysis received from Glen S.:

See below – Series of Radar, tracking incident

Dan's 13 April 2013 Radar FOIA
Allentown PA TRACON
Radar Tracks on Collision Coarse
820 to 920 PM EDT

Unknown Skin Target in BLUE
Aircraft Beacon 4207 in RED
ABE Allentown PA Airport in BLACK
Danielsville PA in GREEN
Lat Long 0.05 Degree Grids

UFO'S – SIGHTINGS---REPORTS - COVER-UPS

820 To 822

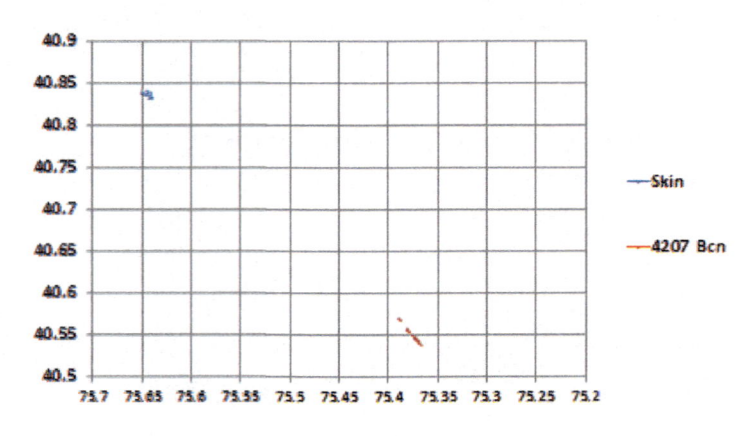

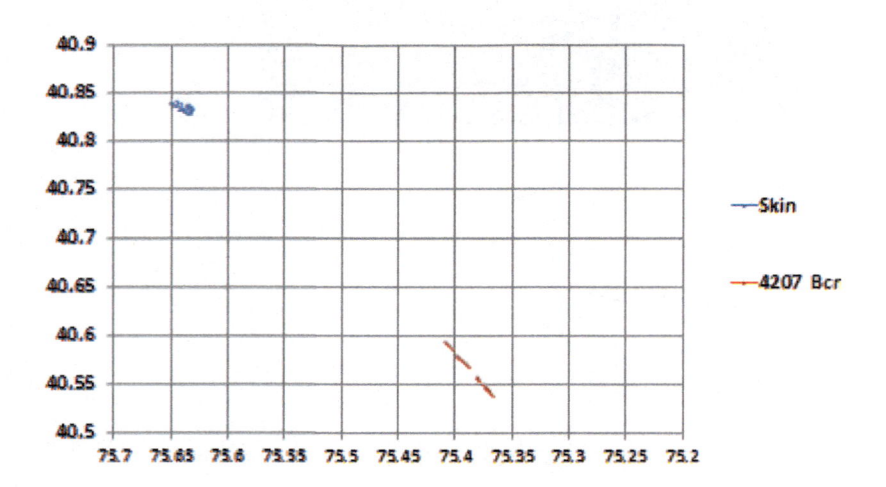

824

826

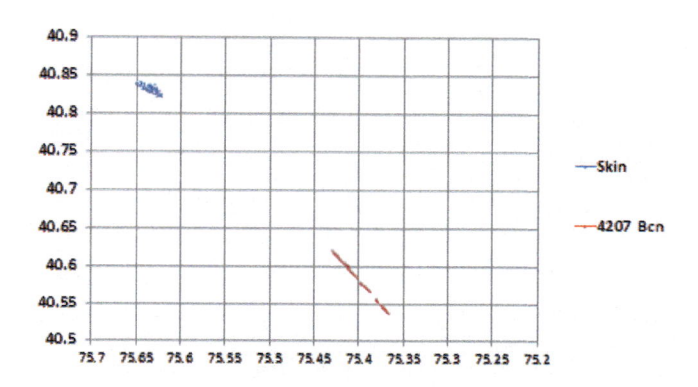

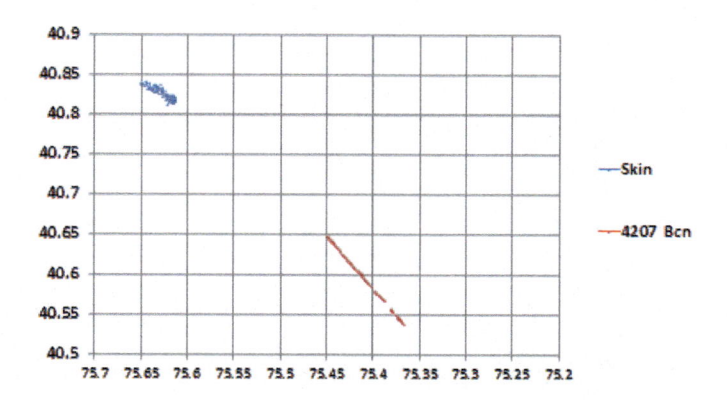

828

UFO'S – SIGHTINGS---REPORTS - COVER-UPS

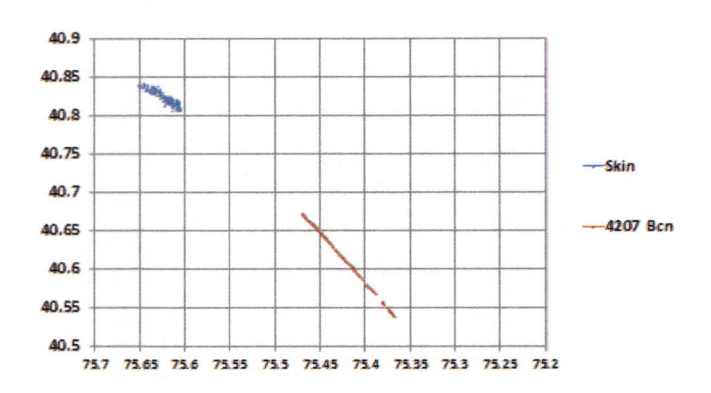

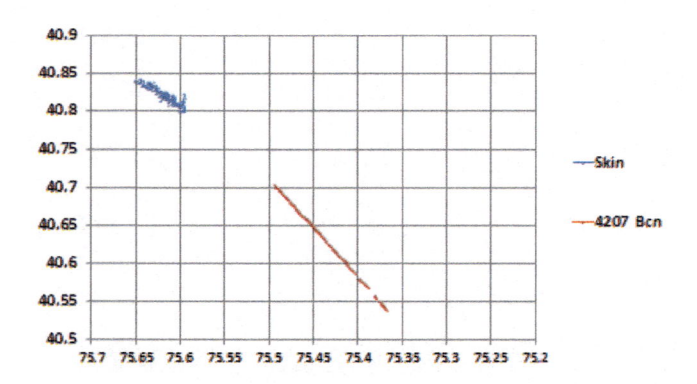

830

832

199

834

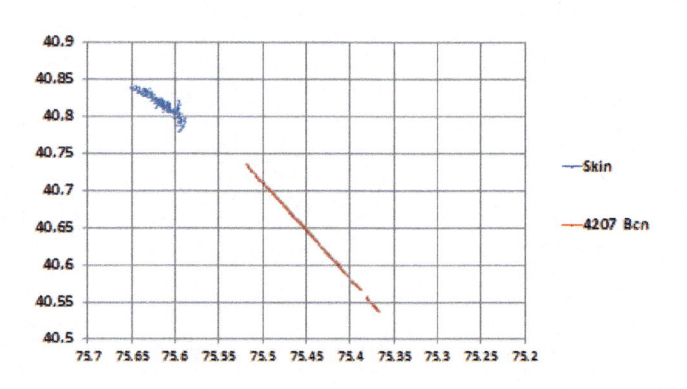

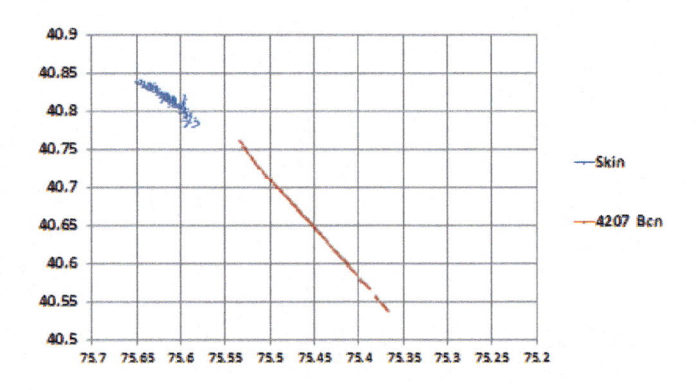

835

836

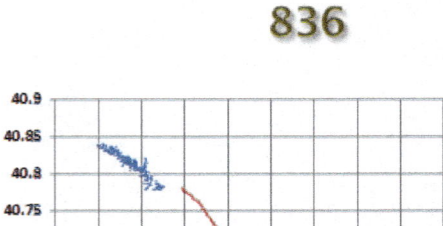

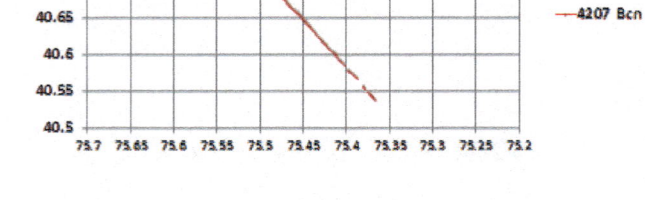

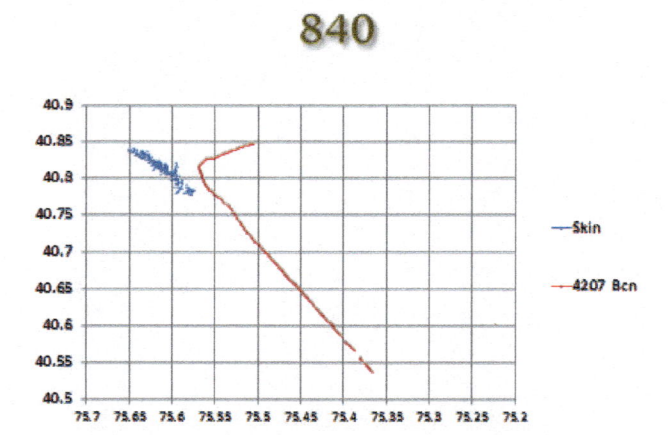

840

845

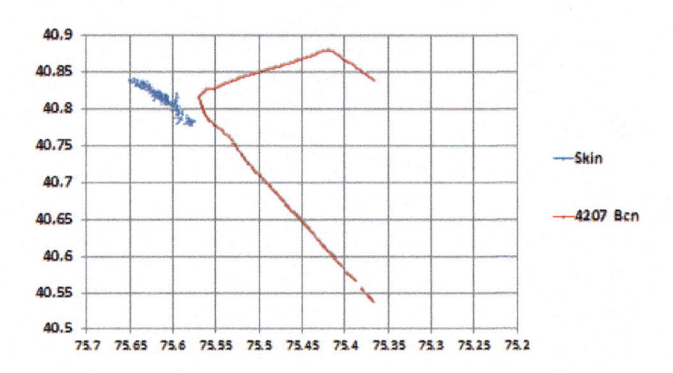

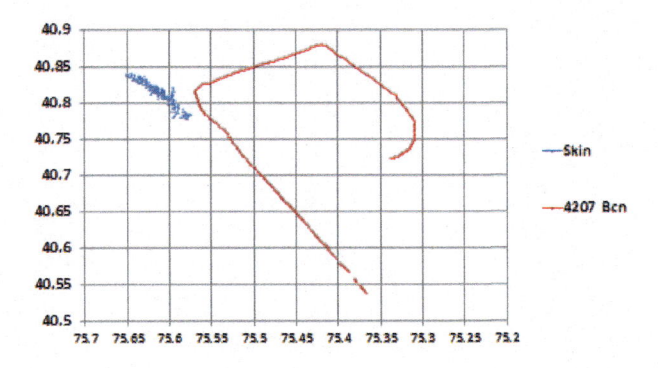

850

UFO'S – SIGHTINGS---REPORTS - COVER-UPS

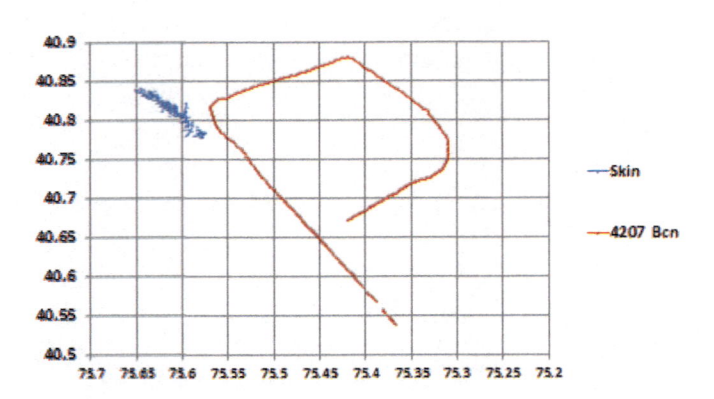

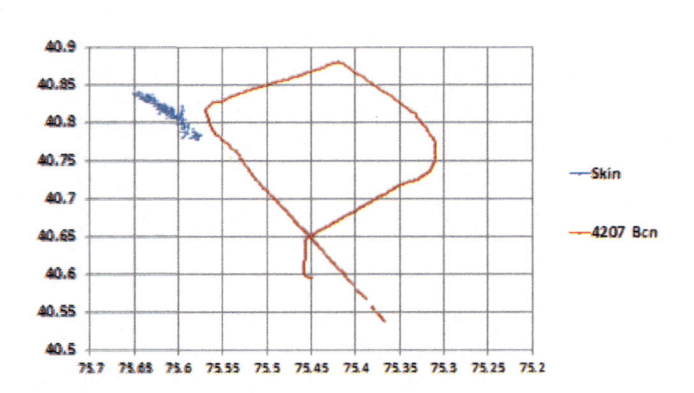

855

900

905

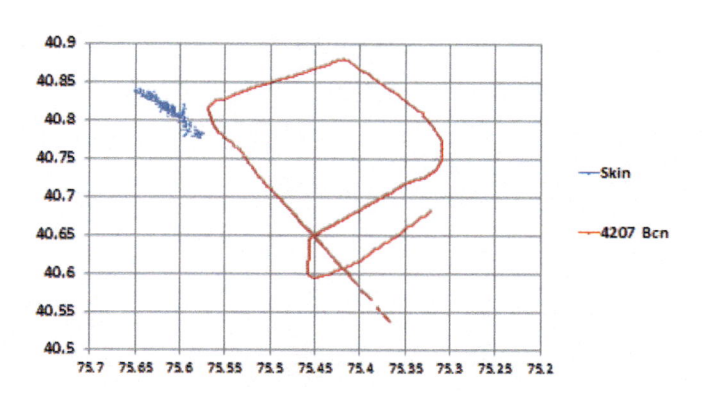

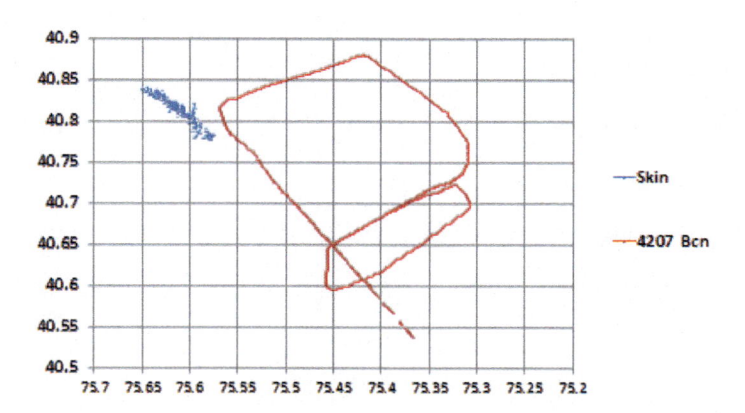

910

UFO'S – SIGHTINGS---REPORTS - COVER-UPS

Glen S. comments on his analysis of radar data received from FAA

1) Two radar targets found on collision headings at 8:20 PM (Evasive action taken to avoid collision at 8:40)
2) Targets @1 Mile Closest Point of Approach CPA at 8:36 PM
3) Skin target goes radar dark between 8:36 and 8:37 PM
4) Beacon Code 4207 changes heading to the east at 8:38 PM
5) Beacon Code 4207 lands to stop at ABE Airport at 9:17 PM
6) Skin target fails to reappear after going dark at 8:37 PM
7) The wide spread pattern of radar returns from the subject skin target places this highly radar reflective object in a size class with the radar returns from large sea-going cargo ships 900 ft by 150 feet in size moving at 10 to 12 knots

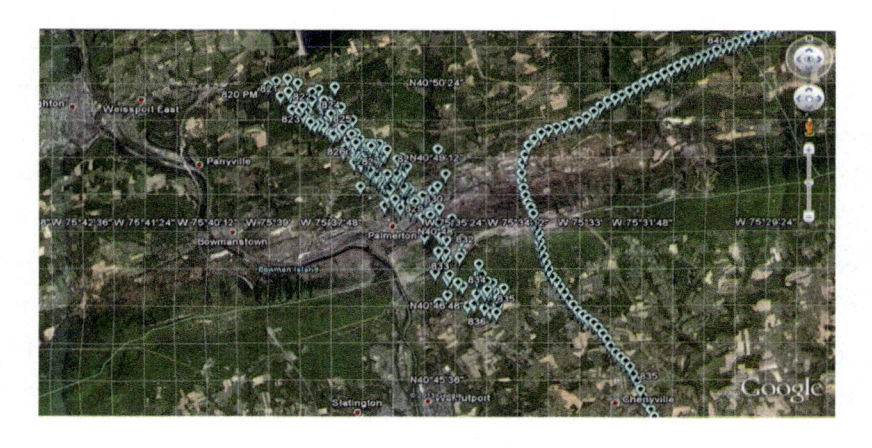

Initial Radar Image shown over map

What took place at this point with respect to the skin paint targets is unclear. An interpretation of the evidence suggests that the objects which were witnessed by the individuals on the ground were probably not the formation that was in the near collision track, but was on the lead edge of at least two formations. The increase in speed described by the witness could coincide with the time of the near collision given that the 8:50 time frame is an approximation. This suggests that both formations might have been in some form of coordinated movement or contact. According to the data supplied, the formations appeared to continue on a southerly course moving at a steady speed of between 10-20 knots until they disappeared from the radar.

UFO'S – SIGHTINGS---REPORTS - COVER-UPS

In continuing the investigation coming up to the end of August, I placed a call into Lehigh Valley Intl Airport looking to talk with tower or airport supervisor. I was able to chat with Airport Supervisor - Tom Stoudt. I explained the information we had on this case and wanted to set up a meeting with him. He asked me to send up the radar data we had, and he would go over it with the tower. Needless to say, I wouldn't be sending up the radar data we had, for fear that it would disappear. I told him that I would bring it with me to discuss during our meeting. He stated that it was the tower that we needed to speak with. He told me that he would touch base with the tower people and advise of our request. He told me either he or the tower would be back in touch with us. I had been waiting to hear back from them for some time now, to set up a visit. Needless to say, I hadn't heard back from anyone at the airport.

In Early September, being that I hadn't heard back from anyone at the airport, I called Tom Stoudt again, wanting to chat with him on our visit status. He wasn't available, so I left a voice message for him. I have been awaiting his call back. Thinking the third time would be charm, toward the end of September, I called Tom Stoudt again, wanting to chat with him on our visit status. He wasn't available, so I left another voice message for him, still awaiting his call back. Which I might add, was never received. Makes you wonder why the airport personnel wouldn't want to address our radar data or questions we had pertaining to it. I would have loved to find out what type of aircraft was reporting back Beacon code 4207. It would have been nice to chat with the pilot of that aircraft and the passengers (if any) regarding the close encounter they experienced.

In parallel, a FOIA request was sent to the National Guard at the former Willow Grove Naval Air Station, Willow Grove, PA, as the unknown objects were traveling south toward the location of this base. Along with this, a "Right To Know" request was sent to the PA State Police. Unfortunately, no State police reports were available from other potential witnesses, who may have observed a possible mid-air collision. The FOIA request that was sent to the National Guard on September 30th was interesting. Dan was inquiring whether the tower located at the Air Guard Station located in Horsham, PA was still active. After several months, Dan finally received an answer in response to the multiple letters he sent regarding the status of his request. The answer came back that the tower at Horsham, PA was inactive. Note: it took several months to tell us this? Makes you wonder why.

Because of the time constraints and lack of cooperation from various resources, this investigation has been documented, saved, and officially closed as a UAV (Unknown Aerial Vehicles).

UFO'S – SIGHTINGS---REPORTS - COVER-UPS

Sighting at Mountain Top, PA – 2016

Mountain Top, PA, is a relatively small suburban community located in Luzerne County, conveniently situated within the I-80/I-81 transportation corridor. PA Route 309 also runs through the area, connecting Wilkes-Barre to the North and Hazleton to the South. Mountain Top consists of Dorrance, Rice, Fairview, Wright, and Slocum Townships. The Crestwood Industrial Park, located in Mountain Top, is one of the region's largest, employing over 3,000 local residents.

It is a popular destination for outdoor enthusiasts, with several state parks, including Nescopeck State Park and Pinchot State Forest, which provides access to the Black Diamond trailhead. Mountain Top is approximately 56 air miles from the northernmost border of New York and approximately 103 air miles from New York City. Trenton, NJ, is roughly 111 miles by car.

Mountain Top, PA, is known for its temperate climate with distinct seasons. Winters are cold, usually reaching temperatures in the mid-30s during the day and dropping down to the 20s at night. Summers are warm and pleasant, with temperatures generally staying in the 70s during the day and cooling off to the upper 50s at night.

A witness (name withheld) who lived in Mountain Top, PA (approximately 18 miles southwest from Wilkes-Barre airport), filed a report on 10/19/2016, stating:

"Around 8:45 pm, I went out on my back deck while my dog was in the yard. I noticed a very bright-looking star that caught my attention immediately. I noted several airplanes flying to the left of this object by a large distance. The object remained stationary in the Northwest sky for about five minutes. I continued watching what I referred to as a star when it suddenly moved downward and took an abrupt turn to the right at a 90° angle in one fluid motion. It paused, tripled in size, becoming brilliant white, and within seconds, took off at a high rate of speed and was gone. The object took off upward and at a slight angle."

UFO'S – SIGHTINGS---REPORTS - COVER-UPS

At that time, as Chief Investigator for Pennsylvania, I had assigned the case on October 19th to one of my trained investigators, Karen C., and State Section Director, Fran I., who was also assigned as backup support, as she lived close to where the sighting took place. This sighting occurred on October 18, 2016, at 9:06 PM E.S.T. The weather was clear and unseasonably warm, with the temperature at approximately 75°F. The sky was also clear, showing plenty of star visibility. There were no satellites, rockets, space junk, iridium flares, or ISS in this region of the sky at this time. Sighting first seen at location: Latitude 41.154569, Longitude -75873644. This is an area located southeast of Fairview, PA, around the Arbutus Peak Mountain of the Appalachian Ridge in Luzerne County.

On October 20th, my investigator, Karen C., contacted the witness to obtain additional information on his sighting. A voice message was left for the witness, who then connected with Karen the following day. During the telephone interview on October 21st, the witness reiterated what he had indicated in his written report. He also submitted a daylight photo showing the Northwestern area of the sky and the surrounding terrain. The two stars marked in dark blue are two familiar stars to the witness (Eyes of Draco: Rastaban and Eltanin). In Red, he marked where the object was and its movement.

Witness photo looking Northwest. Note: Two stars to the left and above the object. The red markings depict motion and direction of the unknown object.

Witness photo looking Northwest. Note: Two stars to the left and above object. The red markings depict motion and direction of unknown object.

In parallel, Karen had contacted the Rice, Fairview, and Wright Twp. Police Departments and also the Hazleton State Police – Troop N, inquiring about any reports of strange lights or sightings. Information she received was that nothing was reported.

As this was a UAP event, Karen completed and filed a FOIA request to the FAA on Oct 26th. A voice message to Karen from the FAA was left requesting additional information on the event. Her reply to the FAA was also left in a voice message on Nov 4th.

UFO'S – SIGHTINGS---REPORTS - COVER-UPS

Radar data usually takes about 6 weeks for process and return, which is normal for the FAA.

Then on Dec 9th, Karen received a package from the FAA. This package contained radar information about the sighting event. The information provided data before, during, and after the event. Not being able to understand what was sent, as the data represented 390,000 radar returns consisting of 244,000 Beacons and 146,000 unknown skin paints. This data was collected from three overlapping FAA ATC antennas: AVP, QRC, and QIE. The AVP is a short-range antenna covering about a 57-mile radius. The other antennas are long-distance radars with a 200-mile reach. This presents a circular track pattern of 400 miles wide.

The data was forwarded to Glen S., a military radar specialist, on December 28th to review and advise on what he had found. The data was received by the analyst Glenn S. on or around December 28, 2016. The area of interest provided for this sighting event consisted of an area of approximately 2800 square miles, in and around the vicinity of Scranton, PA. Initially, the request was for information that covered an area of 30 miles around the Mountain Top, PA, vicinity. The USG FOIA offices sometimes respond with massive overkill in an attempt to confuse and make something unclear, with all the data points provided.

Needless to say, the unknown radar returns and the known returns (response from ATC transponder beacon radar) were received for the requested AOI and TOI for this event.

Transponders are electronic devices onboard aircraft that emit a signal when pinged by radar. This signal tends to identify the type of aircraft and code number back to the radar operator so they know what and how many different aircraft are in the area at a specific time. Data received came from the three ATC operating RADAR overlapping antenna sites.

Site AVP – A TRACON (Terminal RADAR Approach Control). TRACONs are FAA facilities that house air traffic controllers who guide aircraft approaching and departing airports. A TRACON antenna covered four nautical miles east of the centroid of the AOI with a 55 nautical mile maximum range.

Site QRC – An ATC Center antenna located 20 nautical miles west of the centroid of the AOI with a 250 nautical mile maximum range.

Site QIE – An ATC Center antenna located 80 nautical miles south of the centroid of the AOI with a 250 nautical mile maximum range.

The data provided in the FAA response revealed at least 7 non-responsive and non-identifiable highly RADAR reflective "skin paint" objects, which were tracked for 15 minutes plus by their motion in time and space in the AOI and at the TOI. Radar analysis revealed that there were two different groups: a Northern Group and a Southern Group. The Northern Group of unknown radar detected and tracked objects found to consist of at least seven distinct objects moving in coordinated time and space with an orderly separation between them. These objects

UFO'S – SIGHTINGS---REPORTS - COVER-UPS

were traveling to the northeast at 38-40 miles per hour with some tailgating between some trailing objects. The Southern Group of unknown radar detected and tracked objects found to consist of three distinct objects, or one wide-body object moving while maintaining a tightly knit formation in coordinated time and space traveling to the northeast at 38-40 miles per hour. Both Groups transiting the AOI on the same exact heading to the northeast at approximately 38-40 miles per hour. The Groups maintained a lateral north/south separation of approximately 1 mile. Both Groups maintained common headings, velocities, and spacing during the primary radar tracking at 9:00 PM. This is somewhat mysterious and typically unexplainable while occurring in dark skies.

Shown below is a series of the Radar returns for the Southern Group only from the AVP and QRC air traffic antennas, which are separated by 25 nautical miles.

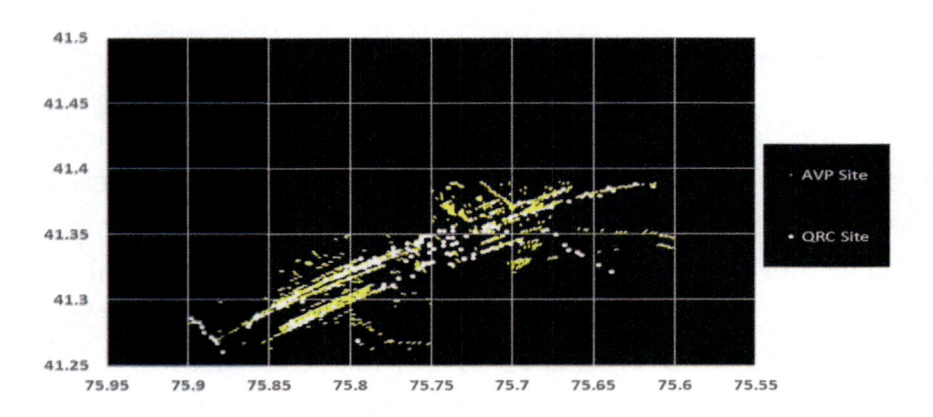

The above shows combined Radar images from the AVP and QRC antennas for the AOI and TOI for the sighting report.

215

When analyzing radar returns, a condition exists where the returns go dark. This is caused when the tracked objects transit overhead through what is called the cone of silence. This is when the objects transit over and above the actual radar site.

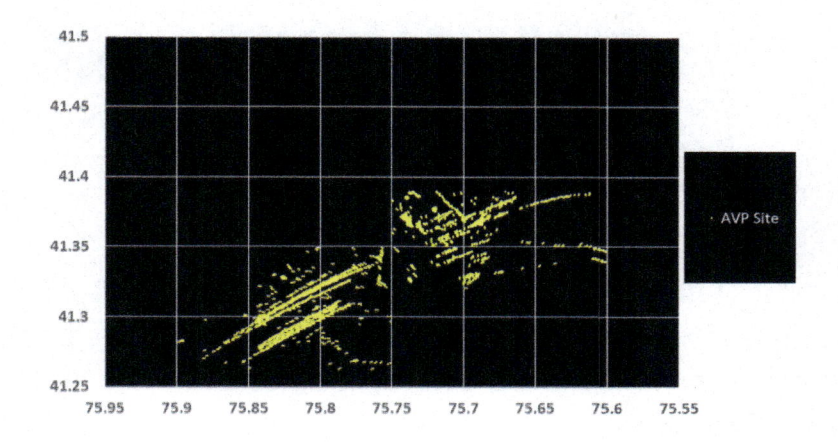

Shown above is the area where skin returns go dark as the tracked objects transit through the cone of silence from AVP

Returns from QRC have been partially decimated by 75% in conjunction with the radar line-of-sight horizon height of 500 to 600 feet AGL at 25 nautical mile range.

Shown below are the QRC skin returns. Notice there is no break in the returns, as these are showing full returns without the radar dark scenario. This is because the returns do not transit above the QRC antenna.

UFO'S – SIGHTINGS---REPORTS - COVER-UPS

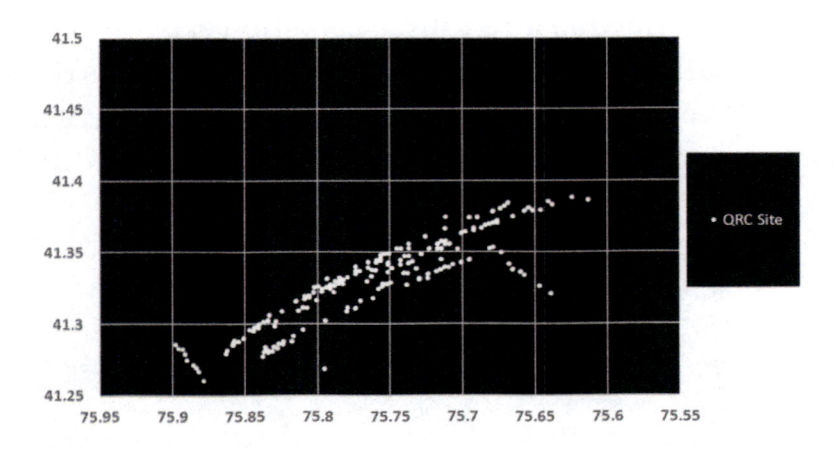

The following slide will show both the AVP and the decimated QRC returns to validate and confirm the continuous skin returns at 25 nautical miles of objects directly in the AVP cone of silence.

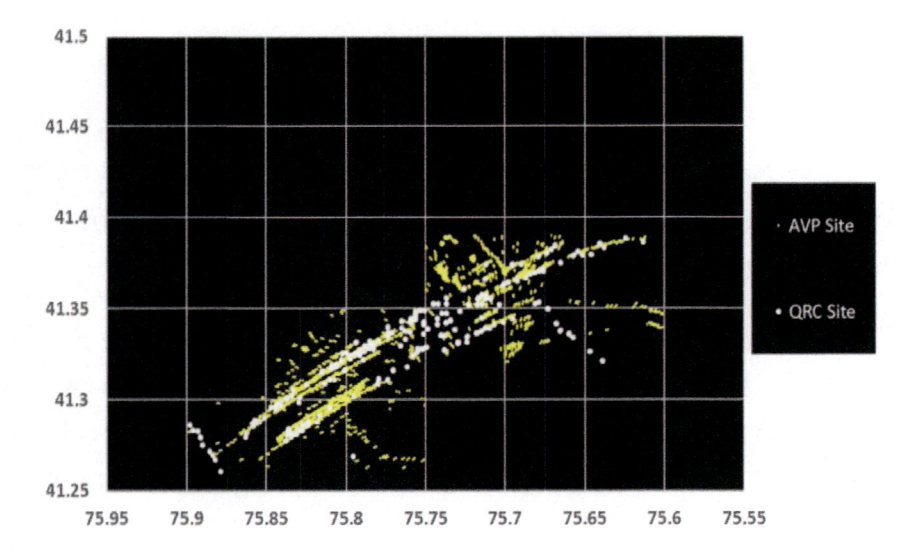

The radar returns had reported a number of skins returns along with a Beacon Return with an ATC code of 5750. This is the signal that was generated from a known onboard aircraft transponder when pinged by the radar. The unknown returns had not provided such a signal and just sent highly reflective skin returns.

The aircraft crosses the confirmed tracks of AVP and QRC skin returns, while the aircraft descends from 4000 feet to land at Wilkes-Barre Airport at 912:20 PM E.S.T. during the 30-minute event TOI.

Show below is the combination radar returns of AVP and QRC with the radar return ATC Code 5750

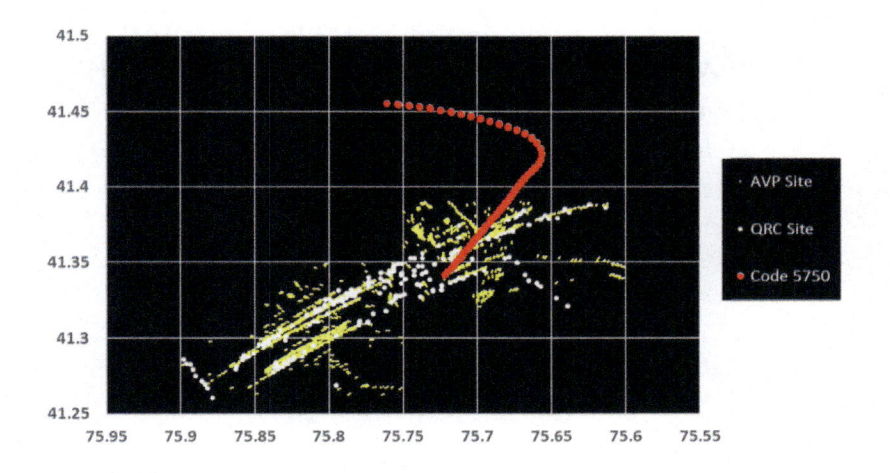

UFO'S – SIGHTINGS---REPORTS - COVER-UPS

The crossing of the skins and the aircraft radar return tracks in the AOI and the TOI produces concerns of a possible ATC near miss event.

It is to be noted that all presented Radar returns are downloaded directly from the FAA FOIA response without distortions, redactions or fabrications.

The RADAR specialist – Glen S. has expressed some concerns about the safety of commercial air traffic in the Scranton / Philadelphia area. The concern is the high number of crossings of RADAR Tracks, which may represent potential near mid-air misses between ATC controlled commercial aircraft and a high number of uncontrolled radar reflective objects moving in time and space. Potentially UFO's

This case investigation has been documented, saved and closed as an "Unknown."

WILLIAM G. WEBER

UFOs & Technology: What Influence Did They Have?

For thousands of years, people have been seeing strange, unknown objects in the sky. Early on, tribes thought they were gods and worshipped them out of fear and wonder. Ancient sites around the world depict them in cave dwellings, tombs, pyramids, and such. We have explored these giant structures, revealing building techniques and alignments that we cannot duplicate today with our modern equipment. Knowledge of the stars and star systems was exhibited as well, with ancient observatories. These structures tracked the positions of the Sun, Moon, and other celestial bodies for timekeeping and the creation of primitive calendars or means to track the seasons.

Stonehenge is one of the earliest such sites or observatories. Ancient astronomers could track the positions of the Sun, Moon, and stars, likely using them to mark significant solar events such as the summer solstice. Perhaps it was used to predict the seasons and determine planting and harvesting times. Where could they have obtained their knowledge of the heavens? Not only this, but how did these people build these structures with the simple tools they had? Some of the large stones weigh more than fifty tons. The inner circle, consisting of blue stones weighing more than four tons, was found to have come from a site over 125 miles away. How did they get there?

It's interesting that experts today acknowledge the axis of Stonehenge is aligned in such a way as to accurately predict the summer and winter solstice.

The observatory at Chichen Itza, located in Central America, is proof that the ancient Maya possessed an advanced understanding of the heavens. They too were able to observe celestial events such as solstices, equinoxes, and phases of the moon. These were instrumental in creating calendars, predicting the seasons to determine planting and harvesting times. The Mayans associated celestial phenomena with gods or spirits. Observatories played a role in their religious ceremonies, sacrifices, and rituals. Today, the Mayan calendar's accuracy is viewed as remarkable. Despite being developed thousands of years ago, it is still considered one of the most precise calendars ever created. The Mayans were able to accurately calculate the length of a solar year to within a few minutes. [1]

Mayans were among the few ancient civilizations who developed an elaborate mathematical system, and they also understood the concept of zero, which enabled them to create their accurate calendar based on solar and lunar cycles. Where did this knowledge come from?

One of the most impressive pyramids at Chichen Itza is El Castillo, also known as the Temple of Kukulcan. **Another pyramid—similar to Egyptian pyramids?** One of the most remarkable features of El Castillo is its precise alignment with the sun. On the spring and fall equinoxes, a shadow resembling a snake can be seen slithering down the staircase of the pyramid, a phenomenon that has come to be known as the "serpent effect." This alignment is a testament to the knowledge and skill of the Maya astronomers, who were able to accurately predict the movements of the sun and other celestial bodies. [1]

Snake shadow

Egypt

The pyramids of Egypt are remarkable structures. We are still trying to figure out today how the massive stone structures were constructed. *Imagine trying to build something like that today with only the simple copper tools they had. Today, where could you find a construction crew tasked to build a pyramid only using these tools?* The ancient Egyptians were avid astronomers. They closely observed the night sky and also used celestial events for purposes like planting crops and harvesting, like the people of Stonehenge and the Mayans of Chichen Itza. Of interest to them was the constellation of Orion. They had aligned the pyramids, which are located outside of Cairo, with the stars in Orion's Belt. Could this be looked upon as a gateway to the stars for the deceased Pharaoh's ascension to the sky, or was this something else? [2]

Pyramid alignment relative to stars in Orion's Belt

Placement of Pyramids relative to Orion's

Stars in Orion's Belt

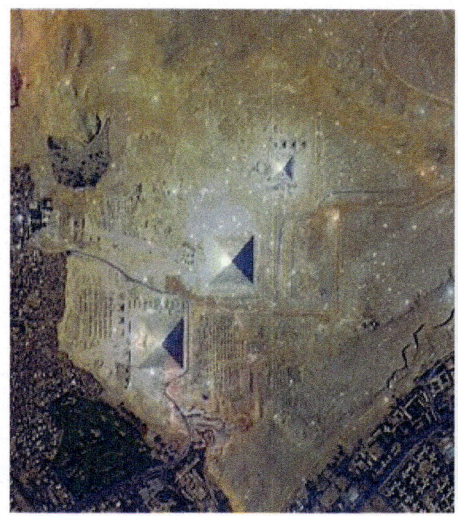

The ancient Egyptians associated their gods with the stars in the sky. According to ancient texts, they believed that Osiris and Isis came down from Orion and Sirius and created all life on earth. They also believed that the gods would come down from the stars one day and live among the regular people.

There has been some thought as to the actual purpose of the Great Pyramid. Rather than just being a tomb for the pharaoh, it was thought to be a power generator, as the pharaoh was never discovered in the pyramid. [2]

This theory is based upon the construction materials—both inside and outside, the passageways, as well as the placement of the pyramid. It was important that the pyramid was placed on the geo-magnetic point of the earth. The base of the pyramid was built upon red granite. All the shafts of the pyramid are built of granite containing large quantities of quartz crystals. Outside the pyramid was covered with non-conductive limestone. Quartz crystal is a very good material for the piezoelectric effect. It is thought that because of the natural vibration of the earth, which is 7.83 Hz, and the weight of the granite, the piezoelectric effect of the quartz would produce microwave energy and electromagnetic radiation, as well as acoustic energy to produce sound through a resonant effect. The great gallery could have been used as a resonator hall. The sound vibrates more, increasing the piezoelectric effect, producing more electricity.

Nikola Tesla studied this and pursued this himself. He wanted to provide free energy in the same manner. To that end, he had solicited funding from several sources. One source was J.P. Morgan. He funded Tesla until he realized the new technology would compromise the existing businesses he was already involved in, causing him to lose money. As a result, he denied any additional funding for the project that Tesla was building in Shoreham, Long Island, NY. As a result, the Wardenclyffe Tower he built was shut down. Tesla ended up a poor man who could have offered the world free energy.

J.P. Morgan, being heavily invested in the rail, rubber, and oil industries, didn't want to compromise them with the introduction of free energy. [3]

Germany

According to various reports that surfaced toward the end of the 20th century, a UFO crashed in Germany's Black Forest near Freiburg in 1936. It is claimed that the craft was saucer-shaped and was ultimately recovered by SS troops shortly afterward. The object was allegedly taken to Wewelsburg Castle, the main headquarters of the Third Reich, where their top scientists, members of the Thule society, worked to reverse engineer it and find ways to use the technology to their advantage. Whether they achieved this or not is open to debate, but it is widely accepted that German scientists and engineers were far ahead of other countries, including the USA, at the time. [4]

The **Thule Society** was founded in 1918. The primary focus was the discovery of the origins of the Aryan race. This was an occult, anti-Semitic, socialist group, which was instrumental in founding the German Worker's Party, which later became the Nazi Party. A Psychic Medium named Maria Orsitsch, also known as Maria Orsic, allegedly had channeling contact with aliens from the Aldebaran star system, **which, by the way, is in a direct line and is pointed to by the stars in Orion's belt.** They were said to have settled on Earth a long time ago in the area of Samaria. It has been said that Orsic allegedly received plans and diagrams through channeling from the aliens, which precipitated building a flying disc. It is alleged that these diagrams and the data from the reversed engineered craft were combined to build the alleged Haunebu flying craft in 1939.

UFO'S – SIGHTINGS---REPORTS - COVER-UPS

Maria Orsic

Haunebu Flying Craft

It was said that there were several versions of the Haunebu flying craft, with more capabilities than the original. They named their latest craft the Vril series. During the war, the Allies reported seeing unknown craft following them or flying alongside the Allied aircraft. These were known as the "foo fighters". **What they were was still unknown.**

Rocket technology progress was developed at Peenemunde, located on the Northeast German Baltic coast. Developed in Germany from 1936 through the efforts of scientists led by Wernher von Braun, it was first successfully launched on October 3, 1942. The V2 rocket designed by Von Braun was deployed and used as a weapon against France and England. When questioned sometime later on how he knew so much about rocketry, it is alleged that he stated, "he had help from them." **Makes you wonder who "them" were.**

The year was 1947 when there was a UFO crash in the desert of Roswell, New Mexico.

WILLIAM G. WEBER

Roswell Daily Record on July 8th, 1947

    Of course, this was downplayed by the government, stating it was a balloon, as usual.

UFO'S – SIGHTINGS---REPORTS - COVER-UPS

Figure 2 Army Denial – Weather Balloon
Courtesy, Fort Worth Star-Telegram Photograph Collection, Special Collections, The University of Texas at Arlington Library

United States

However, there were materials recovered from the craft. These artifacts were glass strands or wires, small wafers containing black chips, pieces of fabric, a flashlight-type pointer, and other material. According to Col. Philip J. Corso (ret.) in his book The Day After Roswell, he stated that he was responsible for the material that was recovered and tasked to find out what this material was. To that end, he had shared this task with some of the larger technology companies in the US, such as AT&T, Battelle, and others. It's important to note that these companies had existing government contracts with the military. Soon after, AT&T/Bell Labs announced the invention of the transistor in 1947/48. This device revolutionized future technology in many different industries. Let's look at some of them.

Note: Prior to the transistor, the technology at the time was electro-mechanical relays, switches, or vacuum tubes. When used for computing, electro-mechanical devices (adding machines) were very slow.

Assortment of Vacuum Tubes

The Electronic Numerical Integrator & Computer – ENIAC (Digital) was an advancement, in that it used a combination of vacuum tubes and relays. It was built by John Mauchly, J. Presper Eckert, Jr., at the Moore School of Electrical Engineering at the University of Pennsylvania during World War II.

The ENIAC occupied about 1,800 square feet with almost 20,000 vacuum tubes, 1,500 relays, 10,000 capacitors, and 70,000 resistors. It weighed over 30 tons.

The ENIAC was completed in 1946. It was 1000 times faster than electromechanical adding machines.

The UNIVAC I - Universal Automatic Computer (Digital) developed by Remington-Rand in 1951, also used vacuum tubes, but far fewer than the ENIAC. It used 6,103 vacuum tubes and weighed about 7.5 tons. It was capable of doing over 2000 calculations per second. It was intended to replace punched-card accounting machines.

Moving forward, solid-state digital technology has advanced at a faster rate. Transistor devices have advanced as well, with the creation of newer, more advanced devices. The technology has grown from simple bipolar devices, up to and including CMOS and MOSFET transistors and Integrated Circuits, that contain several hundred transistor devices. These new ICs offer smaller size and weight resulting in faster calculations and operations with lower power consumption.

Today's Typical Transistor Assortment

UFO'S – SIGHTINGS---REPORTS - COVER-UPS

The Hewlett Packard Enterprise Frontier – Supercomputer, operational in 2022, is the fastest computer in the world.

Because of its high-speed operations, it uses 6,000 gallons of water for cooling. This digital computer can do over a billion, billion (1 x 10^18) calculations per second. This computer is presently located at Oak Ridge, Tennessee, used for scientific research and development.

Because of the invention of the transistor, modern technology had leaped forward in aerospace, defense, communication, automotive, medicine, and commercial industries.

Author's Note: *We've come a long way from the days of vacuum tubes and relays in such a short period of time.*

Getting back to the recovered material...

Battelle, located in Ohio, studied the "metal fabric" and came out with "memory metal" called Nitinol in 1960. Nitinol is an alloy of nickel and titanium that has the ability to return to a predetermined shape when heated. Note: the recovered material on the craft was wrinkled and folded but returned back to its original shape. Applications for Nitinol range from actuators -- solenoids, servo motors, pneumatic valves. Nitinol is highly biocompatible and has properties suitable for use in orthopedic implants and other medical devices such as Nitinol tubing, which is commonly used in catheters, stents, and superelastic needles.

The small wafers that were recovered, which had black chips on them, were sent out for analysis. This eventually led to the development of the integrated circuit.

Integrated circuits today contain many hundreds of semiconductor components, such as transistors, diodes, and all the necessary interconnects between these devices. In fact, a complete computer (micro-processor) can be incorporated into this small package. The first integrated circuit came out in 1958 by a company called Texas Instruments.

Jack Kilby's original hybrid integrated circuit from 1958. This was the first integrated circuit,

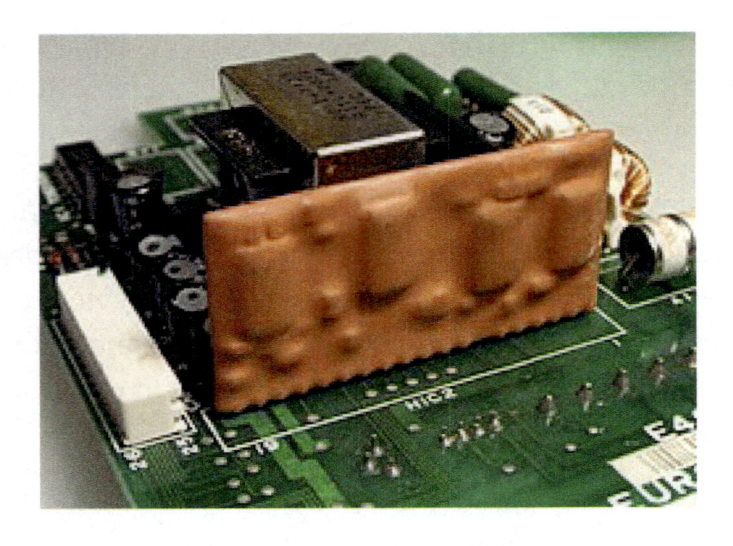

An (orange-epoxy) encapsulated hybrid circuit, shown on a printed circuit board

    A hybrid integrated circuit is a miniaturized electronic circuit constructed of individual devices, such as transistors, diodes, and passive components such as resistors and capacitors that are bonded to a substrate (typically silicon).

Today's Modern Integrated Circuits

This may be hard to comprehend, but there may be more computing power in your cell phone today than what was on the Apollo mission to the moon.

The glass strands recovered led to the development of fiber optic strand material, which was patented by Corning Glass in 1970. An optical fiber is a flexible glass or plastic that can transmit light from one end to the other, which is mainly used in low power situations, replacing more expensive copper.

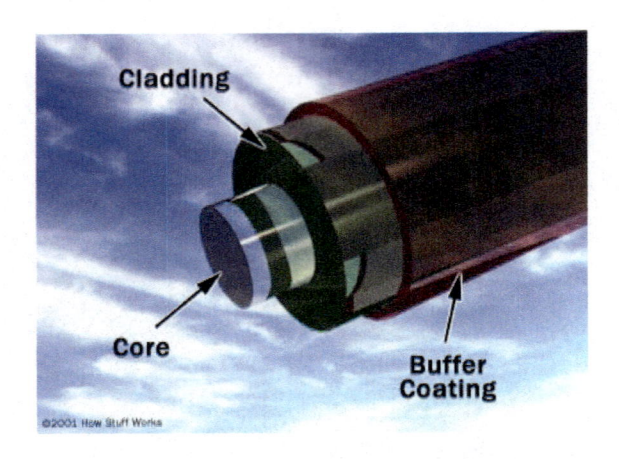

Breakdown of a single optic fiber

The core is the glass or plastic media that carries the light signal through the length of the cable. The cladding contains the signal within the core, thus reducing signal loss. The plastic buffer coating provides protection to the individual fiber strands. There may also be additional strengthening fibers and an outside coating to protect the fiber optic strand.

In communications, fiber optics is widely used for high-speed data communication. Also, fiber optics is used in medical imaging systems, such as endoscopes and cameras. For military applications, fiber optics is used in the main branches of the military for communication and data transmission. There is also a need for low voltage sensing, where fiber optics is used in applications such as temperature sensors, pressure sensors, and vibration sensors. There are surveillance systems using fiber optics to transmit high-definition video over long distances. [5]

As shown, Fiber Optics has real advantages over copper wire in many applications. Needless to say, copper wire has advantages over fiber. These would be in high power situations where the copper would be carrying high voltage or high current loads. There really is a place for both in today's world.

An example of how fiber works in one commercial arena is detailed below: Because they are immune to electromagnetic interference and signal loss when compared to copper wire, companies such as Verizon are using fiber optics as residential cable media (internet and television). This Fiber Optic media product goes by the name of FIOS.

Another one of the recovered articles from the craft was a stubby, "flashlight" sort of device that emitted a very thin light beam. The beam of light was only visible when it went through a smoky atmosphere. Without the smoke, you would only see a red dot, where the "flashlight" was pointed. It was observed that the area the pointed light rested on became hot. The thought was that this was some kind of cutting device or scalpel. [6]

The first Laser was built by Hughes Research Labs. May 16, 1960. Theodore H. Maiman, a physicist at Hughes Research Laboratories in Malibu, Calif., constructs the first laser using a synthetic ruby cylinder. The applications of the laser today, are too numerous to list here. They range from communications, to precise measurements, tracking, surveying, weapon systems and delicate surgery to name a few. [7]

UFO'S – SIGHTINGS---REPORTS - COVER-UPS

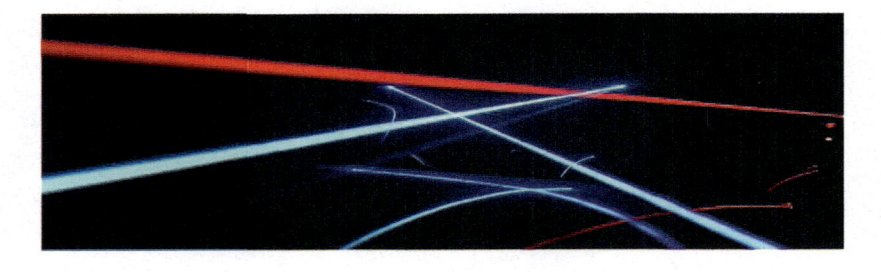

Lasers

In conclusion, with all of the advances that have been made in today's technology, some with our own research and some with the materials that were recovered from a UFO crash recovery, it makes you wonder why the message of denial being fed to us is still the same, even though witnesses have come forward to Congress to defend the proposition that we're not alone.

WILLIAM G. WEBER

The Denial Still Continues

The Department of Defense All-Domain Anomaly Resolution Office

Report on the Historical Record of U.S. Government Involvement with Unidentified Anomalous Phenomena (UAP)

Volume I

February 2024

Conclusion

To date, AARO has not discovered any empirical evidence that any sighting of a UAP represented off-world technology or the existence a classified program that had not been properly reported to Congress. Investigative efforts determined that most sightings were the result of misidentification of ordinary objects and phenomena. Although many UAP reports remain unsolved, AARO assesses that if additional, quality data were available, most of these cases also could be identified and resolved as ordinary objects or phenomena. This report represents Volume I of AARO's HR2. Volume II will be published in accordance with the date established in Section 6802 of the National Defense Authorization Act for Fiscal Year 2023 (FY23) and will provide additional analysis on information not yet secured and analyzed, interviews not yet conducted, and additional avenues of investigation not yet completed by the date of the publication of Volume I.

References

1) theyucatantimes.com/2023/04/the-mystery-of-chichen-itzas-pyramids-techniques-and-theories-behind-their-construction
2) Bing.com/search?q=Are+Egyptian+pyramids+aligned+with+stars
3) https://whatcanilearntoday.wordpress.com/
4) http://10 Outlandish Conspiracy Theories About The Nazis - Listverse
5) https://dgtlinfra.com/fiber-optics
6) From "The Day After Roswell, by Col. Philip J. Corso (Ret.)"
7) www.photonics.com/Articles/A_History_of_the_Laser_1960_-_2019.

UFO'S – SIGHTINGS---REPORTS - COVER-UPS

Glossary of Terms

ABE	Lehigh Valley Int'l Airport
AGL	Above Ground Level
AOI	Area of Interest
ATC	Air Traffic Control - Primary Search Radar
AVP	Wilkes Barre / Scranton Int'l airport
Beacon Code	Aircraft Transponder Code Generator
CPA	Closest point of approach is the situation where the distance between two aircraft is minimal.
DIHEDRAL	The upward angle of a fixed-wing aircraft's wings where they meet at the fuselage
FAA	Federal Aviation Administration
FOIA	Freedom of Information Act
QIE	FAA Radar located near Joliette, PA
QRC	FAA Radar Station – Benton Air Force Station
Skin Paint	Highly Reflective Radar Targets
TOI	Time of Interest
UAP	Unidentified Aerial Phenomenon
UAV	Unidentified Aerial Vehicle
USG	United States Government
ABW	Air Base Wing
NAWC	Naval Air Warfare Center

Printed in Great Britain
by Amazon